D1058984

THE SECRET OF WILDCAT SWAMP

The HARDY BOYS *Mystery Stories*
BY FRANKLIN W. DIXON

"Run for it!" Frank shouted. "The tower has been dynamited."

"Run for it!" Frank shouted. "The tower has been dynamited!"

Hardy Boys Mystery Stories

THE SECRET
OF
WILDCAT SWAMP

BY

FRANKLIN W. DIXON

NEW YORK
GROSSET & DUNLAP
Publishers

CONTENTS

CONTENTS

THE SECRET OF WILDCAT SWAMP

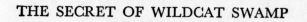

THE SECRET OF WILDCAT SWAMP

CHAPTER I

Prison Break

"IF SOMEBODY doesn't toss a mystery your way, fellows, we may actually be swimming in this pool one of these days."

Frank and Joe Hardy stopped digging and leaned on their shovels. The boys grinned as they studied the perspiring, chubby face of Chet Morton.

"Shall we tell him, Joe?" asked Frank with an exaggerated lift of his eyebrows.

"Tell me what?" Chet demanded. "Aw, listen, fellows, long before school closed for the summer you promised me you'd come out here to the farm and help me clean out this bog. Now you finally made it, let's stick to it!"

Eighteen-year-old Frank Hardy, with a wink at his brother, who was only a year younger, gazed thoughtfully at their best friend.

"Who said anything about quitting?" he observed. "But in the meantime how would you like to help us catch a couple of train robbers, Chet?"

"Wh-what?"

"No kidding!" Joe assured him. "Last night Dad was talking about one of his cases, and said maybe we could help him."

The brothers, sons of Fenton Hardy, an internationally known private detective, often served as assistants to their father. Chet Morton had shared their exciting adventures upon several occasions, but he preferred the enjoyment of a good meal to such strenuous activity.

"Tr-train robbers! Not me! I'd rather dig," Chet retorted.

He sent his long-handled shovel deep into the mire. Then with a heave that revealed a great deal more strength than his rotund figure suggested, he hoisted a load of muck and shale from the bottom of the bog to the high ground behind him.

"Say, look at that shale you just tossed up!" Joe exclaimed as his quick eye noticed part of Chet's last shovelful landing on the bank. "It cracked open, and there are funny-looking marks inside it!"

Curious, Frank picked up a piece of the shale and inspected it more closely.

"Looks like indentations from old clamshells, doesn't it?" he remarked. "Wonder how they got there?"

"Oh, you find all sorts of queer marks on rocks

and things which have been under water," Chet answered knowingly. "That's nothing at all. Throw the silly thing away and let's get on with this job!"

A new voice interrupted him. "Wait! Don't throw that away. It's valuable."

Turning, the three boys discovered Thomas "Cap" Bailey, popular track coach and science teacher at Bayport High, standing on the rim of the excavation. Still in his middle twenties, he therefore was not much older than his students, who had high regard for his record as a former captain in the Air Force.

"That's a brachiopod!" he exclaimed, examining the piece of shale in Frank's hand.

"A w-who?" Chet stuttered.

"It's a valuable fossil—maybe millions of years old," Cap reported with a smile at his student's puzzlement. "They turn up every now and then in different corners of the world, and scientists use them to trace the development of man and animals through the ages."

Crouching down beside the boys, he showed them what a perfect specimen the brachiopod was.

"You ought to take this down to our Bayport Museum, Chet. I doubt that there's one like it in their collection."

Chet's barrel chest swelled. "Good thing I shoveled that out of this bog," he remarked in what was meant to be an offhand manner. "It might have stayed under here for another century or two!"

Frank nudged Joe. In a loud stage whisper, he asked of no one in particular:

"Who was it, a couple of minutes ago, that was telling me to 'throw the silly thing away'?"

Chet's sputtered reply was interrupted by Cap, who spoke directly to the Hardy brothers.

"How would you fellows like to combine some detective work with fossils?" he asked.

"I knew it!" Chet moaned. "Here goes our pool. It'll never be finished now."

Frank and Joe eagerly questioned their science teacher for more details.

"Just a week before school closed," he said, "I received a letter from an old aunt of mine out West. Her husband, Alexander Bailey, died recently, just when he felt he was on the verge of an important discovery."

"Was he a scientist, too?" Joe inquired.

"Yes, a geologist. It seems that about a year ago he uncovered part of what appeared to be a giant fossil, and from his previous experience he decided it was a prehistoric camel that once roamed the western United States."

"A camel!" Chet gulped. "Did Indians ride 'em?"

The only answer he got was a solid dig in the ribs from Joe, who was nearest, as Cap went on, "Soon after my uncle's discovery one of those terrific western storms hit the spot and completely obliterated all of his work. Then he was taken ill and did not recover."

"Too bad," Frank murmured.

Chet, still hoping to keep the Hardys working at his project, asked how Cap's aunt expected him to find the camel when it was covered up.

"I haven't told you all the story," Cap replied. "Before he died, my uncle scratched out a rough map of the section, with the location of his original discovery indicated on it. He called the place 'Wildcat Swamp.' "

That was all Chet needed. "Wildcats!" he exclaimed, and concentrated his attention on the excavation job.

His shovel fairly flew as he tried to ignore any more of the conversation, but under his breath the others could hear him muttering:

"Train robbers—wildcats—swamps—ugh!"

"The reason my uncle called the place Wildcat Swamp," Cap Bailey went on, "was that not far from the site of his discovery he had found a sign reading: 'Here lie the bodies of twenty wildcat.' "

"That's strange," Joe remarked. "The killer must have been a mighty hunter."

Bailey nodded, and considered his two young friends. "I guess anyone going into the area would have to keep his eyes open. And, incidentally, I've already found out there is some danger to even starting for the spot."

"What do you mean?" the boys chorused.

"Well, after school closed I started for Wildcat Swamp alone, in my car. I hadn't made any secret about my trip. Any number of people must have heard me talking about what I intended to do. But I hadn't driven far from Bayport when I was held up by two masked men and all my money stolen. I was told to go back home and stay there."

Frank weighed the coach's words thoughtfully. "You think they meant to discourage you from going after the fossil?" he asked.

"Of course I'm not positive, because they didn't mention the fossil specifically, and didn't take the map. That might have been because another car came along just then. But they seemed to know who I was, and mentioned that it would be healthier for me in the East than out West."

"It does sound as if they wanted you to give up the idea of that trip," Joe commented. "But why? Their language sounds more like thugs than that of scientists."

Cap Bailey nodded quietly. "A mystery already. The reason I came out to see you two Hardys," he said, "is this: How would you like to make the trip with me! We all know one another pretty well, from classwork and from our track activities, and I think you could be a big help. What do you say?"

Frank and Joe hardly had to look at each other to confirm their enthusiasm.

"It sounds wonderful to me," shouted the impulsive Joe. "Let's get ready. How soon do we leave?"

Frank was just as receptive to the idea of adventure as his brother, but slightly more realistic in his approach.

"Three of us together should certainly be able to handle more trouble than one man alone, but first we'll have to get Dad's and Mother's okay."

As it turned out, that was no problem at all. When they reached home, their quiet, pretty mother said she would leave the decision to their father. After the situation had been explained to him that evening, the tall, well-built detective said with a smile:

"I think such a trip would be good experience for you boys, and besides, it might even work in with the case I asked you to help on."

"You mean the train robbers? How?" Frank asked.

"I had Sam Radley, my best operative, tailing a fellow named Gerald Flint for some time after he was released from Delmore Prison. Once Sam overheard Flint use a phrase that sounded like 'twenty wildcat' in such a way that he's sure it has some special significance. And now Flint has disappeared."

"Wow!" Joe cried. "You don't mean he's in Wildcat Swamp?"

"I wouldn't go that far," his father answered.

"But a good detective never misses a clue. If you boys can find out more about the 'twenty wildcat,' it may help me."

Cap Bailey was pleased to hear the brothers could go with him.

"I'll give you a couple of days to pack up," he told them.

Next morning, at their father's suggestion, Frank and Joe paid a visit to Warden Duckworth at Delmore Prison. The officer was a friend of Mr. Hardy's, and he gladly spent some time telling the boys about Gerald Flint, an old-timer with a long record. Flint was described as a big, loudmouthed man, who could be soft-spoken and persuasive when he wanted to be.

"His best friends here at our prison," the warden remarked, "were Willie the Penman and Jesse Turk. Willie's real name is William Mogul, but no one ever calls him that. He's a little scrawny fellow with a high-pitched voice, and one of the best—or worst—forgers in the country. He was released at the same time as Flint."

"What about the other fellow—Turk?"

"Jesse is still here. He's a mountain of a man—a former locomotive engineer, and an expert electrician, but not too popular. He has a mean look about him—always frowning at something."

Frank and Joe were just bidding the warden good-by when they heard a sudden clanging, followed by the deafening roar of a siren directly overhead.

"There's been a break!" Duckworth shouted. "Stay where you are, boys, or you may get into a line of fire!"

A moment later the telephone on his desk added to the din. As Duckworth lifted it, Frank and Joe could hear excited chatter on the other end of the line. The warden turned to the boys, his eyes popping.

"It's Turk—he's escaped!"

CHAPTER II

A Dangerous Chase

HIS face grim, Warden Duckworth ordered his car,
then dashed from the office.

"Come on, Frank!" Joe cried, starting down the
long, low-ceilinged corridor.

"I wonder how Turk ever got out," Frank said,
racing after his brother.

Reaching the outer prison yard, they saw guards
everywhere, on alert with rifles in case more of the
prisoners should try to take advantage of the confusion and make a break.

"I was told," Duckworth said to the man at the
gate, "that Turk may have escaped by jumping into
a butcher's truck as it left the prison. Did you see
which way the truck headed?"

"Yes, sir. North on Route 403. It was a National
Meat truck."

Three emergency trucks came roaring to the gate
from the prison garage, followed by the warden's

car. As the Hardys climbed into it, Duckworth advised them to remain at the prison, but they assured him that they would keep out of harm's way.

At his direction, the trucks split up outside to comb the countryside. Individual armed guards tramped on foot in search of the fugitive, while the motor crews toured the near-by roads.

"Best thing for us to do," Duckworth instructed his driver, "is to follow 403."

The route passed through a sparsely settled wooded section for several miles before it entered a town of any size. The tires of the warden's car squealed as it took the curves at almost full speed.

"Do you think the truck driver planned this with Turk?" Frank asked.

"I'm not sure," the warden replied. "Usually an escape involves more than one prisoner. I'd be more inclined to think—"

"Look!" Joe cried. "There's a delivery truck ahead. I think I can make out the name. Yes, it's a National Meat truck!"

"You boys stay below windshield level," Duckworth ordered. "I'm going to force him to stop. It wouldn't surprise me if the driver is Turk himself. If so, there may be trouble. Get down!"

With a burst of speed, they raced past the truck, sounding the siren. With no attempt at resistance, the driver slowed and came to a stop.

Warden Duckworth jumped out, gun in hand.

When the butcher's driver saw the gun, his jaw fell. "What's the big idea?" he shouted.

"You may be carrying an escaped prisoner!"

The driver went white as the warden approached the rear doors of his truck and flung them open.

"If Turk was ever in here, he's gone now," Duckworth said disappointedly. "I'll radio the other men."

Frank and Joe got out and spoke to the truckman. "Do you mind if we have a look inside your truck?"

"Go ahead."

Climbing into the cool interior, the boys began examining it carefully for clues to the missing convict.

"Here's something," cried Frank almost immediately, as he picked up a small wooden box. "Why, it looks like some kind of homemade radio set."

It proved to be a miniature receiving set, so small that it fit snugly in the palm of Frank's hand. As he turned a knob, the gadget began to sputter.

"Repeating Turk," it suddenly announced. "Freight delayed. Hook 138576 at three Rock Spring."

As suddenly as it had begun, the voice broke off.

"That sounded like Flint's voice!" shouted the warden. "I'm sure that was Flint!"

"But what did all the gibberish mean?" queried Joe. "Was Flint in on Turk's escape?"

"Might have been," Duckworth retorted tersely. "Turk worked in the electrician's shop in the prison and took several courses in radio mechanics while he was there. He may have rigged up this communications system as part of a planned break."

"So when Flint and Willie the Penman got out they could tip him off on how to get away," Joe suggested.

"That's the way it might have worked," agreed the officer.

" 'Freight delayed. Hook 138576 at three Rock Spring,' " Frank repeated. "Sounds as if a railroad freight may be part of the plan. You said Turk was a locomotive engineer at one time, didn't you?"

"That's right!"

"I don't know what 'Hook 138576' could mean, but three Rock Spring might mean time and place. It's almost three o'clock now—and Rock Spring isn't far from here!"

"Let's get moving. Rock Spring in a big hurry!" Duckworth shouted at his police driver, and they scrambled aboard for the mile and a half drive to the railroad line.

"There's a water tower on the line at Rock Spring," Joe recalled. "But the road doesn't go in that far, Warden."

"We'll have to make the last half mile on foot."

Reaching the end of the bumpy country road, they all jumped out of the warden's car and headed for the rail line. Frank and Joe, still in good condition from track work during the spring, soon outdistanced the others. But before they reached the right-of-way they could hear the heavy thunder of a freight train.

"Maybe we're too late," Frank said, puffing. "Hey! Here comes a car numbered 138576! I'll bet that's what the message meant!"

Before Frank could answer, the car had rumbled past them. Suddenly the sliding door of the boxcar began to glide open. Then, as car 138576 moved still farther ahead of the boys, a large, well-padded hook was extended from the interior.

"Look, Frank!" Joe shouted. "That man!"

Out of the bushes alongside the right-of-way dashed a burly figure. Timing his sprint perfectly, he pulled up just as the hook reached him. With a desperate grab he caught it, and was immediately drawn inside the car. The freight thundered on.

"That must have been Turk!" Frank exclaimed.

By the time they reached the rails, the caboose had rolled by. The boys ran along the track behind the caboose for a short distance. There was no trainman in sight to hear their shouts or see their frantic signals.

Minutes later, Warden Duckworth and the driver caught up with them. Frank breathlessly explained the strange getaway of the fugitive they believed to be Turk.

"I'll phone from my car," the warden said, "and have the freight searched at the next station."

Contacting the prison, he asked the operator to relay the message to the railroad authorities. Then they drove back and waited in his office for word. When the report came, it was discouraging. The railroad police had opened car 138576 at the next stop, ten miles ahead, but had found it empty.

"Turk and his buddy inside must have seen you boys and were smart enough to sense that someone was on their trail. They must have left the train somewhere along the stretch between where Turk got aboard and the next town. But we'll catch up with Turk somewhere. Prisoners don't break out of here and stay out—very long!"

The Hardys remained in the warden's office for a while, hoping that there would be further news of the fugitive. When none was forthcoming they agreed that they should get home as quickly as possible and tell Mr. Hardy of the escape of Turk.

"This convinces me that Flint is up to his old tricks again," Mr. Hardy said. "But to what extent I can't tell. All I do know is that there has been a series of freight train robberies throughout the country, and it's up to me to figure out how to put a stop to them."

"Who engaged you to take this case, Dad?" Joe asked.

"The North American Railroad League. That's

a group of railroad executives. They've been losing a lot of property in train robberies, and believing that the various thefts were the acts of a single gang of bandits, they think I can break up the racket."

Mr. Hardy then went on to explain that the robbers, so far as he had been able to find out, had used either of two methods in their plan of operation.

"Sometimes," he said, "they throw a road block at strategic points, where the engineer can't see it in time to stop his train. In this way they create wrecks and make their hauls during the confusion.

"At other times they manage to send false messages by radio, and induce the train crew to switch certain boxcars to specified lonely sidings. Then they just move in and loot them."

"Sounds like a pretty slick outfit," Joe remarked. "They seem to have their organization well lined up."

"Yes, they have. That's what makes them so tough to handle," his father affirmed.

"Dad," Joe asked, "do you suppose the phrase 'twenty wildcat' is some kind of password?"

Frank, who had been listening quietly, offered an additional idea. "It's possible that the railroad thieves have some kind of headquarters near where Cap's uncle was digging for the fossil. Maybe a cache where they hide their loot."

"That would certainly account for their not wanting any strangers in that immediate territory," Mr.

Hardy agreed. "They may have been trying to discourage Bailey by holding him up on that first trip. As a matter of fact, they probably planned to steal the map his uncle left."

The Hardys spent another half-hour considering various angles to the case, then the boys' father said he must get some papers ready for a flying trip to New York.

"I'm getting the eleven-o'clock plane, so I'll be there first thing in the morning for a conference with the League officials," he explained.

After a taxi had taken Fenton Hardy to the airport, the boys discussed their own trip, and the clothes and equipment they ought to take.

"I suppose we'll be on horseback a lot of the time," Frank remarked.

It was nearing midnight before the brothers had their gear packed. They were about to start for bed when the telephone's shrill ring disturbed the peace of the big, frame house.

Frank answered the call, as Joe stood near by. A woman's voice, edged with hysteria, said:

"This is Mrs. Bailey, Frank. I've already called the police, but I think you should know what has happened here."

"What, Mrs. Bailey?"

"Two masked men broke into our house and ransacked it. They attacked my husband and left him unconscious!"

CHAPTER III

A Hazardous Take-off

IN LESS than five minutes Frank and Joe were racing through Bayport's dark streets toward Cap Bailey's home.

"I hope Cap's not badly hurt," Frank said worriedly.

Joe's only answer was a nod of agreement. He was concentrating on piloting the speeding car.

By the time the boys reached the Bailey house, the police already had arrived. Frank and Joe dashed up the steps and were immediately recognized by the officer on duty at the door.

"Might have known you fellows would be on hand sooner or later," he said with a grin. "Where's your dad tonight?"

Explaining that Mr. Hardy was on his way to New York, Frank asked about Cap Bailey's condition.

"Oh, he's all right now. Nothing serious," the

18

policeman assured them, and motioned the boys inside the house.

Cap was sitting on the living-room sofa, holding his head, Mrs. Bailey beside him. A police sergeant was conducting the investigation, and Cap was telling him the details. He was glad to see the Hardys, and after a few brief words with them continued his account.

"My wife and I had just returned from a concert, and I had gone upstairs," he reported, "when I heard her cry out. I ran down and found her struggling as she was being tied up by one of the masked men. The other held a gun on me and told me to stand with my face against the wall. A moment later I felt a blow on my head, and that's all I know."

His wife took up the story. "After that they turned the house upside down, searching for something. They must have been almost an hour at it. Cap was just beginning to stir again when they finally left, and I managed to struggle free."

The police officer checked again with Cap. "Have you looked over your things to see if anything is missing?" he asked.

"Yes, but nothing much is gone. Only a duplicate map I've been making for a trip I plan to take this summer, but it wasn't complete."

Frank and Joe looked at each other with understanding. The map of Wildcat Swamp!

"They didn't get the original?"

"No, I had that well hidden. You see, Officer, it's a map of some property out West, that may have some value to it." With the promise that nothing would be made public, he told the sergeant some of the background of the situation.

Meanwhile, another policeman had been searching the entire house for clues of any sort that might have been left by the housebreakers. Now he came up to his superior.

"Sarge, we may be able to get some prints off that back kitchen window. It looks smudgy—unless the marks were made by one of the family."

"No, I washed every window in this house today," Mrs. Bailey asserted. "There were no smudges on any of them."

Hopefully, the police lifted all the prints they could find, and finally left the house. The Hardys' offer to remain overnight, in the event that the housebreakers might return, was welcomed by Mrs. Bailey, even though Cap thought it unnecessary. The boys, after calling home to let their mother know where they were, took turns sleeping, but there was no further visit from any prowlers during the night.

At breakfast Frank and Joe discussed the night's adventure with Cap as they stowed away some of Mrs. Bailey's crisp, brown waffles. Both boys questioned the science teacher closely as to how many people might be aware of his intended trip.

"As I told you, it was no secret at all," he replied.

"Matter of fact, a reporter from the Bayport *Times* got wind of it and came around for an interview. He wrote a long article for the paper."

"Good night! Did he mention the location of Wildcat Swamp?"

"No, I didn't tell him that. But I did mention the sign that my uncle had found, and the words 'Here lie the bodies of twenty wildcat.' "

Their conversation was interrupted by the ringing of the telephone. Cap answered it, and came back to the table looking pleased.

"They have a clue to one of the men," he remarked. "They were able to trace those fingerprints on the window to some character named Willie the Penman."

Frank and Joe almost shouted. "Willie the Penman! He's that friend of Flint and Turk," Frank exclaimed. "Now we know there's some kind of hookup between Dad's case and this new business!"

They told Cap and his wife about the series of train robberies which Mr. Hardy had been engaged to investigate, and also about the prison break in which Turk had escaped from Delmore.

"I wonder if Willie or someone else in the gang happened to see that story?" Joe ruminated.

"He could have," Cap said, "although I hardly think he's the type who would be interested in paleontology."

"It certainly begins to sound as if Wildcat Swamp

might be a hide-out for escaped criminals, with Turk joining up with Flint and Willie the Penman," Frank observed.

"I take it you fellows are still interested in making the trip?" Cap asked with a grin.

"More so than ever," Frank cried. "The further you get into a case like this, the more it gets under your skin."

"All I ask," Mrs. Bailey interrupted with a worried glance at her husband, "is that you all take care of yourselves. I'm afraid that these men may be very desperate characters."

Joe, who had been silent for several moments, now came up with a new approach to the problem. How would it be, he suggested, if they made the trip by plane instead of by car?

"We could even set out for a fake destination, to throw those guys off the trail in case they try to follow us," he proposed.

Cap and Frank weighed the suggestion and found it thoroughly practical. It would be faster and would cut down time and lessen the opportunity for interference.

"Green Sand Lake might be the ideal destination to announce for public consumption," Cap remarked. "It's well known as a searching area for fossil deposits, and it's only about three hundred miles from Bayport."

From there, they agreed the three could go by rail to a place closer to Wildcat Swamp. There they could procure mounts and make the final stages by horseback. But this phase of the journey they would hope to keep a secret.

Breakfast over, the brothers went off to arrange details for this new jaunt. First they contacted Jack Wayne, a private pilot who had become Mr. Hardy's right-hand man on charter flights. Jack was delighted to accept the assignment, especially when the boys gave him a sketchy outline of the reason for the trip and told him not to let the word get out where they were going.

At home, though, they ran into trouble. During the boys' brief absence, their Aunt Gertrude, who lived with them, had returned from a visit and had taken over on the home front. An elder sister of Mr. Hardy's, this energetic woman had a determined air and an eye that missed little, yet the boys were very fond of her and liked to tease her.

"Going away again I hear," she said as the brothers were carrying their gear down the stairway and out onto the porch. "Fingerprint sets, radio sending and receiving sets. Where are you going, the Antarctic?"

Patiently but hurriedly they told her of having been asked to act as bodyguards and detectives for their science teacher, Cap Bailey.

"Bodyguards!" the elderly lady ejaculated. "Aren't they the ones who always get shot first when someone is going to be assassinated?"

"Don't worry about us, Aunty," Joe said, grinning. "We'll duck between the bullets. And we need the radios so we can keep in communication with the undertakers just before the assassination."

With a gasp, Aunt Gertrude threw up her hands, saying she was sure the trip would come to some strange end.

Take-off time was set for early the next morning. Though the Hardys were at the flying field long before the time of departure, Chet Morton was there ahead of them, greeting Jack Wayne and bringing the travelers a box of candy as a parting gift.

"It's only what I would like someone to bring me," he remarked when they thanked him. "And I wouldn't have to be going away, either," Chet added, eying the candy box with a hungry look.

"All right, all right, let's open it right now," Joe said with a laugh. "Help yourself, Chet."

"Why, yes, I will," he remarked, casually removing as many as one hand would hold. "And if you fellows need any help out West, just call on me. Well, I'd better hurry back to the swimming pool. So long."

He drove off and the three travelers climbed into the cabin of the low-winged silver plane. Jack turned the switch and pressed the starter button. The big paddle-bladed propeller became a transparent disk.

Frank and Joe had flown with Jack Wayne many times before. They admired the way he handled his

plane, *Skyhappy Sal*, and the carefree smoothness
with which he flew her.

After warming the engine to the proper temperature for a take-off, he swung the ship into the wind
and lined up on the north-south runway, which
paralleled the entrance road.

"All set?"

The three passengers nodded, and Jack shoved
the throttle forward. The powerful engine roared,
and the plane rolled ahead. As they gained speed,
the runway flashing below the windows, suddenly
the plane gave a lurch.

Jack yanked the throttle back and the engine's
roar died. But their speed was still high, as he eased
in the brakes. The next instant a heavy jolt shook
Skyhappy Sal. Frank, sitting on the left, saw something dart from beneath the wing on his side and
bound away.

A wheel!

It rolled onto the road, just missing a car, and
causing it to swerve dangerously out of line.

In the cockpit Jack Wayne fought to keep his
careening aircraft from reaching the road and over-
turning. Desperately he threw all his weight on the
right brake. There was a loud, grating splatter as
dirt flew up over the windshield.

CHAPTER IV

Fingerprint Trap

JACK's passengers clung desperately to their seats as the tilted plane spun and skidded through the soft earth. Inches from the busy roadway it came to a halt. There was a moment of silence.

"Great work, Jack!" Frank found his voice.

Cap slapped the pilot on the shoulder, as Joe added his praise. Only Jack Wayne's great skill had kept the plane from turning over and had saved the Hardy boys and Cap Bailey from being injured.

"This is a tough accident," the track coach said. "How did it happen?"

"The retaining collar slipped off," Jack replied, after examining the landing gear. "But I can't understand why. A cotter pin holds the collar tight and that keeps the wheel on the axle. I checked the plane this morning. There wasn't anything wrong with that wheel."

Frank, Joe, and Cap looked at one another, the

same question in each one's mind. Had someone tampered with the plane because of them?

"Jack, would it be hard for a person to loosen one of these wheels?" Frank asked.

"Any good mechanic would know how," the pilot answered. "Why?"

Frank told him of the attack on Cap. It was entirely possible that someone had taken this fiendish method of trying to stop the trio from making the trip.

"I guess we'll have to travel by train after all," Cap said.

"Nothing of the sort." A determined gleam came into Jack Wayne's eyes. "I'll get another plane. Perhaps the airport manager will let me borrow his. We shan't be delayed more than fifteen minutes."

His confidence in the friendly airport manager was not misplaced. After hearing their plight, he readily offered the use of his private plane. The travelers transferred their equipment at once.

Again Jack taxied to the runway, warmed his engine, and lined up for the take-off. This time the plane rolled smoothly down the hard surface, rose into the morning air above Bayport, and headed for Green Sand Lake.

Presently Joe found himself admiring the unlimited view. In the clear air he could spot landmarks he knew were twenty-five, even thirty miles distant. He could even make out another plane, a mere dot on the horizon behind them. Ten minutes later the plane was still there, exactly the same distance away.

"Frank, do you think that pilot could be following us for no good reason?" he asked.

Craning his neck, Frank scanned the horizon to their rear.

"How long has it been in sight?"

"Long enough for me to become suspicious," Joe replied.

"What's the matter, boys?" Cap spoke up.

Joe explained, then told Jack. "How about slowing down and letting him pass?" he suggested. "Maybe we can identify him."

Jack throttled back but so did the pursuer, remaining far to the rear. All the boys could discern was that the plane was a low-winged, single-engine type similar to their own.

At length Jack Wayne eased off his power and slanted down for a flawless landing on the small Green Sand airport. The plane behind them made no attempt to land, and soon disappeared in the distance.

"Guess we were mistaken about that fellow," Cap observed, as they unloaded the baggage. A few minutes later the pilot wished his passengers good luck and started back for Bayport.

Green Sand airport was a desolate spot in rough country several miles from town. It boasted one large frame building, a sort of combination hangar and administration shack.

"I'll try to arrange some transportation to the fossil area," Bailey said.

He walked into the building, leaving the Hardys in charge of the luggage. A few seconds later Frank, peering upward, said:

"Here comes another plane. And from the make it *could* be the one that was following us."

The trim, low-winged craft droned around the field, making its traffic pattern. Then the blaring engine quieted and the ship floated in to a fast landing.

The pilot taxied in front of the boys, whirling his ship around and blasting them with a dusty slip stream. He cut the switch, and without so much as a nod, walked off to the hangar.

The stranger was a tall man with slick black hair. But his eyebrows were surprisingly light, which made his eyes seem like black marbles. His nose looked like a bony blade stuck on his thin face.

"Sociable guy," Joe said with a wry grin.

"Don't like him," Frank said crisply. "Did you notice his walk?"

"Queer," Joe agreed. "He slithers like a . . . well, like a snake. I wonder who he is."

"You couldn't find out from his plane," Frank observed, walking closer to it. "The identification numbers are practically weathered off."

"Or rubbed off on purpose," Joe suggested. "And say, look at that little insigne on the cowling."

"A snake," Frank whispered. "A snake eating a bird! It fits the fellow all right."

A fuel truck rolled toward them. As it drew closer, the boys discovered that the beak-nosed pilot was riding with the driver. He alighted and strode up to the Hardys.

"What's the idea of snooping around my ship?" he demanded.

"We were just looking it over," Frank said casually. "We wondered how you can fly it without license numbers."

"That's none of your business," the man snapped. "It's due for a new paint job at the end of this run, since you're so worried about it. Now I'll thank you to move on."

He turned to the gas-truck driver. "Get me a taxi," he said.

The driver nodded, completed his refueling job, and rode off with the pilot. At the same moment Cap Bailey pulled up in an old-fashioned rented car, and the boys put the luggage on its roof. They set off, following directions to the fossil area. Twenty minutes later they reached the famous spot.

"The sand really has a greenish look," Frank observed.

Cap smiled. "You'll find that the study of fossils is pretty interesting. Paleontologists who dig them up are the detectives of the past, and fossils are their clues. You can tell from them what the climate was; if the place where they lie buried was dry land or ocean. The land we're standing on was once deep beneath the sea."

"This far inland?" Joe remarked.

"Even farther. That's why Chet found a seashell in the middle of a hayfield. This green sand was left behind by an immense sea that covered the eastern part of the country many centuries after the bra-chiopods died. By the way, this sand makes very good fertilizer."

"Like cheese, eh? When it's green, it's ripe!" Joe quipped.

"Another interesting fact fossil hunting teaches us," Cap went on, "is that the farther back you go in history the larger the animals were. Right here in the United States there once roamed the largest animals in the world—dinosaurs, and flying reptiles with a wingspread of twenty-five feet."

"Man didn't have much chance," Frank ob-served.

Cap smiled. "It wasn't too long ago that certain scientists thought they had figured out how tall prehistoric men must have been."

"You mean by comparing them with the ani-mals?" Joe asked. When Cap nodded, he said, "How tall were Adam and Eve?"

"Adam was one hundred twenty-three feet, nine

inches tall. Eve was a comparative midget. Only one hundred eighteen feet, nine inches."

"Wow!"

Bailey grinned. "It's a good thing other scientists found bones of prehistoric man to *disprove* it."

The conversation turned to more serious matters. Cap asked the boys if they felt sure they had eluded any pursuers interested in stealing his map of Wildcat Swamp.

"I don't trust that pilot who flew in right after we did," Frank answered.

"Since we seem to be watched," Joe said, "maybe we ought to rig up a booby trap."

"What kind?" Cap asked.

"Well, if I were after any papers of yours, I'd figure they were in that brief case you carry. Let's take out what's important and leave the brief case in the car. Then we can walk out into the dry lake, circle around, and watch."

"Good idea," Frank agreed.

"And in case someone takes that brief case, how about a little of that powder we have in our pack, Joe?"

Frank opened one of the bags and took out a plastic tube.

"What is it?" Bailey asked.

"A special dye powder. We'll sprinkle it lightly over your brief case. It's the same color as the leather, but if anyone gets it on his hands, a green stain will show up in a few minutes. And he'll have a terrible time washing it off."

"We may not catch the villain red-handed, but we'll sure catch him green-handed," Frank chuckled.

The trap was laid quickly and the car parked in plain sight. The three worked their way across the dry lake bed, around boulders, and through scraggly stunted brush, until the car was out of sight behind a low hill.

"Now let's hurry to the top of that hill and wait," Frank urged.

But before they could reach the top a voice hailed them, "Hey there! What are you up to?"

Cap and the Hardys stopped in their tracks and turned. A uniformed policeman had dismounted from a horse and was hurrying toward them.

"I've been watching you," the officer puffed. "You don't act like fossil hunters to me. I patrol this area every day—lots of them perfessor guys get lost out here—but you ain't fossil men. You ain't even got any equipment."

"No, we're not here for fossils," Cap admitted. He told the policeman of the trap they had just laid and why. "Will you help us?" the teacher asked.

The policeman became interested. "Hm. Sounds exciting, and nothing exciting ever happens out here. My inspection's over. I'll go along with you. But don't try any funny tricks."

He plodded behind the others up the low hill and crouched with them in a clump of thick brush.

"Hope we don't have to wait all night," the officer said. "It's nearly sundown now."

"We won't have to wait at all," Joe whispered excitedly. "Look!"

There was a movement in the weeds near the car. Suddenly two men stood upright, glancing about furtively. Then, swiftly and silently, they moved to the car and opened a rear door.

CHAPTER V

Into Perilous Country

"Don't jump them yet!" Cap Bailey hissed at Frank and Joe as they started to leave their hiding place. "Let those thieves commit themselves!"

The two men snooped around inside the car for a moment or two. Then one of them picked up the brief case and began to paw through its contents.

"Now!" yelled Cap, and the Hardys and their new police aide sprinted from cover.

Four to two, they soon had the invaders under control, although both were big men, one of them a huge, strong-armed fellow. The policeman's uniform and gun had a quieting effect on the situation, however.

"What were you fellows looking for?" Cap demanded.

"Nothing," the larger of the intruders muttered sullenly.

35

"W-we're just hungry and thought there might be some food in this car," the other man offered, but it sounded like a spur-of-the-moment excuse.

"Looked to me like you had a pretty good idea of what you wanted," the policeman said suspiciously. "And it wasn't food."

"I'm sure you're right," Frank agreed. "Can we get these fellows into custody around here?"

The officer quickly produced two sets of handcuffs from his saddlebag, and directed the way toward the local country jail. Then, asking Joe to ride his horse behind the car, he ordered the two snoopers onto their hands and knees on the floor in the back of the car. He sat on the rear seat between them with his gun out and ready for action.

Cap and Frank occupied the front seat, the boy driving and Cap facing around to aid the officer in case of trouble.

The jail was five miles away, but it did not take long for them to cover this distance, even proceeding at a pace slow enough for Joe to canter along behind. Reaching the small wooden structure which served as town hall and jail, they all went inside.

"We didn't do anything. You can't hold us!" the big man exclaimed stubbornly when they were arraigned before the local magistrate. "For all we knew that car might have been abandoned. We were just wondering if we could help the owner."

"Yeah, help him out of anything that belonged

to him," the policeman snorted. "I saw you going through the brief case, buddy."

"We'll have to hold you," the magistrate decided. "Names, please."

"Uh—Jake Johnson."

"And Jim—er—Jones. How long you gonna hold us?" he growled.

Frank and Joe pulled Cap into a huddle a short distance away.

"Listen, Cap, the shorter chap looks just like a picture that Dad showed us of Gerald Flint," Frank whispered.

"And the other guy sure fits the description of Jesse Turk—a man-mountain if ever I saw one," added Joe.

Cap considered. "We don't want to let them know we suspect them, because we're not sure they know who we are," he decided. "How about getting fingerprints from your father and Warden Duckworth?"

The trio called the magistrate aside, explaining their suspicions and the necessity for hiding their identity for the time being.

"I can't hold them without a warrant," the officer told them.

"We can prove enough on them now to give you cause to hold them until the prints arrive," Frank said.

Going over to the huge man, he asked him to

hold out his hands. Unsuspectingly, the man complied.

"You see that green stain on his hands?" Frank asked the magistrate. "That came off the brief case belonging to this friend of ours. I dusted that brief case with a special chemical powder before we left the car. It's proof this man was handling it."

Snarling like a couple of trapped animals, the suspects were led away to small cells in the rear of the building.

The brothers put in a long-distance call to Bayport and informed their father of what had happened. Fenton Hardy, delighted that his sons had outwitted the men, promised to have the prints sent to the Green Sand authorities overnight.

"Now for Wildcat Swamp!" said Joe elatedly, as they left the jail.

"Let's see, from here we can get a train as far as Red Butte," Cap remarked. "We'll return the rented car, buy our tickets, and eat supper on the train. We ought to get into Red Butte by morning, and we can get our ponies and supplies there."

They enjoyed a good meal in the diner, and discussed plans for suitable equipment to be carried in their packs when they switched to horseback. It was still early morning when they arrived at their destination, and Cap thought they had better use the hotel as a temporary headquarters. He led the way to Red Butte's only hostelry, the Silver Saddle.

"Breakfast for three, hey?" the bewhiskered clerk greeted them. "Sure, we can take care o' ye." Learning they had come by train from the East, he said, "Have ye heerd all about the big news up to Green Sand? Sheriff Paul was just in here tellin' me about it."

Frank nudged Joe, smiling, and Cap grinned too.

"Fust time I ever heerd of anybody breakin' out that there Green Sand jail," the old man went on in his squeaky high-pitched voice.

Frank's head came up with a start, and Joe and Cap snapped to attention immediately.

"What do you mean, break out? Did someone get away?" Joe demanded.

"Why, shore, that's what I'm a-talkin' about," the clerk retorted. "Two fellas, just stuck in there yestiddy for stealin' outta someone's car, busted clear out last night! Got clean away!"

The three travelers looked at one another gravely. Turk and Flint—if it had been they—were on the loose again! Another dire thought struck the Hardys and Cap. Would the men pick up their trail and show up at Red Butte to make more trouble?

After some deliberation, the trio decided to leave as soon as possible for Wildcat Swamp.

"While we are waiting for breakfast, I think I'll send a message to Dad," Frank said. "He ought to be kept informed of what's going on. Suppose you buy camp provisions while I contact him."

"Okay," Joe and Cap replied.

Fearing that a public telephone might be inadvisable, Frank hired a room and hooked up the powerful little radio set. Switching to the secret frequency used by the Hardys, he called his home.

Back in Bayport Fenton Hardy became disturbed when he heard of the desperadoes' escape, and said he would set certain wheels of justice in motion immediately. He agreed that there was nothing for the boys to do but to proceed to the swamp as planned.

Meanwhile, Joe and Cap had finished making their purchases, and had returned.

After a nourishing breakfast, the three went out to purchase the digging implements they would need. At the general store the obliging clerk said:

"Since you're headin' into dangerous country, I'd advise you to take along pistols. Only last week a trapper shot an ugly wildcat out there."

"Thanks for the tip," Joe answered. "Do we need permits?"

"Not for pistols carried in plain sight."

"Then we'll buy three."

"Now we'll have to see where we can rent some horses," Cap Bailey said. At the livery stable to which the clerk directed them, they were able to hire three sturdy saddle horses and a strong pack mule.

By midmorning they had packed their camping gear onto the mule and were ready to take off. Cap and Joe took the lead, with Frank bringing up the rear holding the animal's lead rope.

"Wildcats, here we come!" Joe cheered as they cantered from the main street of Red Butte into the desolate-looking country southwest of the town.

"By my figures, according to Uncle Alex's map, it will be a good twenty-five miles to the swamp," Cap called from up ahead. "And this is pretty rugged country!"

That was, at best, a mild description of the terrain through which the riders now passed. Following, in general, a swift little stream that wound back and forth through the uneven, rocky ground, they criss-crossed this brisk rivulet again and again. The sun rose and the dusty air became scorching.

"We won't reach the first landmark until some time tomorrow morning," Cap commented when they stopped for lunch. "That will be a big tree near the ridge of a small mountain."

"Any kind of a decent-sized tree would look good to me," Joe said, perspiration soaking his khaki shirt. "You sure can get tired of looking at this brush, and sand, and rocks."

"Cheer up!" Cap laughed. "When we get deeper into it, you'll find hills and small mountains. According to my uncle's map, the section around Wildcat Swamp is really up-and-down country."

By late afternoon the extremely slow, steady plod-ding had brought them to a more fertile area, with scattered trees and more lush grass. The long trek had taken its toll of riders and horses. All were tired, irritable, and jumpy. A wild rabbit, exploding into flight almost under the front hoofs of Frank's weary mount, sent the horse rearing and would have precipitated a nasty spill except for the boy's excellent horsemanship.

"Listen to those coyotes howl," Joe muttered. "They're the spooks of the prairie, all right."

"We'd better not go more than a couple of miles farther before we bed down for the night," Cap advised. "Once the sun goes down out here, it gets dark fast." A short while later he called a halt.

"I'll take a look around while you get the supper started," Joe said with a grin at Frank, whose turn it was to prepare the meal. He wandered off through the underbrush.

Meanwhile, Cap busied himself getting the bedrolls unpacked and feeding the animals. Frank soon had their own simple supper ready. They were about to summon Joe when he suddenly began shouting to them from some distance away. It was a desperate call for help.

"Frank! Cap! I'm caught in quicksand! I'm sinking!"

CHAPTER VI

A Wildcat Attacks

"QUICKSAND!" Frank yelled, and Cap echoed the dire word.

Dropping a panful of steaming beans unheeded into the fire, Frank flipped a coil of rope off his saddle, and he and Cap raced in the direction from which Joe's shouts were coming.

"Over this way!" Frank directed with a yell as he caught sight of his brother beyond a cluster of low bushes. "But be careful where you step!"

Cap took one look and called advice to Joe, who had been sucked in up to his thighs and was sinking rapidly.

"Hold still! Stop trying to kick loose!" the coach shouted. "You're only digging yourself in deeper!"

By this time Frank had found the edge of the mire, and braced himself on the nearest bit of solid ground. With a quick heave, he sent one end of the rope looping toward his brother. Joe made a frantic grab for it.

"Wrap it around yourself and hang on!" Cap commanded. "We'll pull you out."

Together, he and Frank began hauling on the sturdy hemp. Stiffening his body, Joe was slowly dragged up and out of the sucking, oozing sand, and at last lay panting on the hard, firm ground at their feet.

"Whew!" he whispered as the strength began to return to his legs. "That was close. I couldn't do a thing to help myself."

Frank and Cap sat down beside Joe until he had recovered sufficiently to walk back to camp. Still shaken by the experience, they had little appetite for supper. Their campfire was only a bed of coals when they returned.

"Before it gets too dark, we'd better check over our equipment and get the horses hobbled for the night," Cap spoke up finally. "The bedrolls are laid out, but I didn't do anything else."

Frank volunteered to lead the animals to the edge of the stream which had been their guide all day, and he let them drink all they wanted. Then, after tethering them, he stepped back into the little circle of light made by their rekindled campfire.

"All set for the night," he announced. "Hope it doesn't rain."

"Not much chance," Cap predicted. "Look at

those stars. You certainly don't see them that bright back in the city, do you?"

"Almost bright enough to travel by," Frank remarked. "But say, what's that other light off there to the left?"

All three stood up and studied the distant glow. As they watched, it flickered, and seemed to move from place to place.

"It must be a fire of some kind," Frank decided. "Someone else is camping out here—maybe Flint and Turk."

"I doubt it," Cap disagreed. "The way the fire moves, or seems to, I'm more inclined to think it's a swampfire than a campfire. A campfire, from this distance, would give a pretty steady light. A swampfire is bright in one spot for a minute, then flares up in another."

Joe, impulsive as ever, immediately forgot his misadventure of the early evening. "Let's ride over," he proposed.

It was the work of only a few moments to bank their own fire against spreading, and throw saddles on the horses.

Keeping well apart and permitting their mounts to pick their own way in the darkness, the trio moved toward the strange light.

"It's a swampfire, all right," said Joe. "But— look!"

He was first to notice the figures of several men

crouched around one small blaze. "That's a camp-fire!" he whispered to his companions. "There must be half a dozen men there. And horses, too."

His own mount had discovered the presence of other horses, and now let out a loud whinny. Immediately excitement broke out around the camp-fire. The men scrambled to their feet, ran to their horses, mounted them, and rode away. It all happened within the space of a moment's time.

The Hardys would have followed them, but Cap forbade this because of their unfamiliarity with the territory. They did inspect the camp, however, but found no clues other than the hoofprints.

"Did you notice that one of the riders went off alone?" Joe asked the others. "I wonder why. The rest of them beat it in the other direction."

"Here are the marks of his horse," Frank said, turning his powerful flashlight on the ground. "Small hoofprints, too, as if it were only a pony, and probably carrying a very light rider."

"Are you thinking what I'm thinking?" Joe interrupted him. "Willie the Penman?"

"Could be," was Frank's terse answer. "And say, the prints lead in the direction of Wildcat Swamp!"

"You're right!"

"We can't be too careful the rest of our trip," Cap warned as they made their way back to their own camp site. Nothing had been disturbed, and although each was curious about the mysterious riders, his curiosity did not prevent him from dropping off to sleep.

Joe was first awake next morning, and whipped up a solid breakfast before rousing the others. They paid another brief visit to the mystery camp before setting out for Wildcat Swamp but gleaned no further information than they had in the darkness of the previous evening.

"It won't be long before we ought to start looking for that big tree mentioned on the map," Cap spoke up. Since early morning the three travelers had come quite a distance from the camp on the plain.

They were in hill country now. The trail wound up and down through rugged terrain with patches of woodland becoming more frequent. They rode along the rim of one small canyon and through the dry bed of another. After considerable time had gone by, Cap said:

"I certainly expected to see that big tree by this time. If Uncle Alex was right, we should be in plain sight of it, and there's nothing here but this scrubby pine."

"There's no sign of a big tree but that old stump over there a short distance from the edge of the ravine," Frank said, pointing. "Looks as if it had been a whopper, too."

Joe jumped off his horse to examine it, while Frank and Cap checked the map.

"Maybe we haven't gone far enough," the science teacher said. "Once we get out of this sandstone area, there ought to be quite a stand of tall yellow pine."

They were interrupted by a shout from Joe. "Come here! This isn't an old stump. It's new. The tree has just recently been cut down!"

When the others reached him, Joe was scraping away at the top of the stump.

"Look, this has been covered with mud to make it look like an old cut," he exclaimed, and clawed a handful of dirt away to reveal comparatively clean, new wood underneath.

"But where's the tree?" Cap demanded.

Frank looked over the edge of the ravine. "Down there," he announced.

The others stood on the rim and stared into the canyon. There lay the big pine, its larger branches sheared off, and thrown in beside it.

"Someone must have wanted to remove this tree mighty bad," Cap at last broke the silence. "What a job it must have been to roll it over the cliff."

"Do you think it was done to destroy our landmark and cause us delay in finding the swamp?" Joe asked.

"It looks like it," Cap agreed. "The tree certainly was cut down within the last couple of days, maybe only yesterday."

"By the men we saw at the campfire last night, I'll bet," Frank conjectured.

"How about the map that was stolen from you back in Bayport—the unfinished copy? Had you put the tree on that?"

"Yes. That was one of the details I had drawn on it."

Frank stared at the teacher. "Then I'm sure, Cap, it was an attempt to remove something we've been counting on to help us find Wildcat Swamp."

"We may as well go on that assumption," he agreed.

So the trio pushed on, stopping only a short time to rest their horses and eat a quickly prepared lunch.

As they rode through the heat of the afternoon, Cap asked the boys if they had noticed the formations that looked like giant toadstools made of clay and sandstone.

"Yes," Frank answered. "I was wondering what keeps them from crumbling down. It's the column underneath that seems to be made of clay, with the big mass of sandstone up on top."

"It's the overhang which prevents the clay from eroding," the teacher told him. "Back in the glacier age, they were separate deposits, and all the clay except that protected by the sandstone has eroded."

Joe was impressed by the colors of the huge sandstone tops. "Cream, buff, gray—I even saw a couple that looked light green," he remarked.

"As we push deeper into rougher country, you'll see a lot more of the various layers that have covered this section," Cap commented.

Rougher country was not long in coming. The riders wove in and out of the rocky ridges, their respect for their sure-footed horses increasing as they proceeded.

Frank was in the lead, with Cap next and Joe bringing up the rear with the mule. The cavalcade skirted the edge of a deep ravine, the trail following a bench that dipped gradually toward the stream below and ending in a narrow grassy shelf. Suddenly Frank called out that he could see another giant stump at the edge of the shelf.

Permitting the horses to graze on the scanty grass, they went to examine the stump. Frank was about to remark that this was an old cut, when Joe's voice rang out in alarm.

"Frank! Look out!"

But his warning was too late. Before Frank could even get his arms up to defend himself, a tawny streak of fur and muscle launched itself through the air from the rocky overhang above.

It was an enormous wildcat!

....
....

CHAPTER VII

The Spiral Code

THE big cat was in mid-air before Frank was even
aware of it. He had no time to defend himself.

As the beast leaped at the boy, his horse, with
animal instinct, reared and screamed. The horse's
split-second movement distracted the cat and gave
Frank time to recoil a step, so that it missed its
target and sprawled on the ground beside Frank.

Crack!

The sharp explosion came from behind him, and
the wildcat sank to the ground. Another quick report, and the snarling, spitting beast lay lifeless.

Frank turned to see Joe, his gun still smoking,
looking coolly at the still form of the lion. Finally
he raised his eyes to his brother's face.

"Now we're even, Frank," he said. "This makes
up for getting me out of that quicksand yesterday."

Cap broke into a relieved chuckle and remarked
to no one in particular, "I certainly knew what I

was doing when I picked you boys as bodyguards!"

After making sure his attacker was dead, Frank turned it over.

"Mangy-looking beast, isn't it? Say, I wonder if this is the breed of wildcat the swamp's named after."

"I don't know," Cap admitted, "but if it is, I'd say the hunter who killed twenty of them was mighty handy with a gun."

Frank grinned. "Like Joe here."

After pushing the carcass over the cliff, they took up the trail again.

"This is the longest twenty-five miles I've ever ridden," Joe remarked after a while. "It seems as if I'd been in the saddle a month."

Cap admitted that they had made slow progress, but he felt that they had done well enough considering the difficulties of the trail they had to follow. Late in the afternoon they came to a spot where he suggested they make camp.

"We'll be leaving the stream at this point," he told the boys, "and we might as well hole up where we're sure we'll have water."

"What happens to the stream?" Joe asked.

"According to Uncle Alex's map, it cuts through a narrow plateau, and then winds around and down into Wildcat Swamp, which is almost due west from where we are. We'll pick it up again down there."

Once more Joe took charge of hobbling the animals, and watched with sympathetic understanding as they stood up to their hocks in the cool, swirling stream.

Cap and Frank busied themselves with starting a fire and making preparations for supper. While gathering dead branches for firewood, Cap suddenly let out an ejaculation of surprise.

Running to his side, the Hardys found him poring over a narrow strip of paper, evidently torn off a larger piece.

"I found this stuck on that bush over there. I wonder whether it was dropped by a person passing by or whether it was left for someone to pick up. It has writing on it in indelible ink, but in a most peculiar style."

Frank examined the characters, which were arranged as follows:

```
HA    RD    YTR    AIL    HO    T    OFF
B     R     US     H      B     OYS
```

"It's some sort of code, I'm sure," he said. "Let's see if we can figure it out."

Joe had been looking at the strange paper over his brother's shoulder.

"Say, let's see that," he said excitedly. "I've an idea!"

Pulling a pencil from his pocket, he wound the thin strip of paper up its length. The letters suddenly fell into place.

HARDY TRAIL HOT BRUSH BOYS OFF.

In dismay, Cap looked at Frank and Joe. Some-one was well aware of their presence in the area, and was giving orders to have them kept away—if not seriously harmed!

Frank guessed what the teacher was thinking. "Now that we're being watched, all we have to do is turn the tables."

"That's right," Joe agreed.

Cap was not fooled by their bravado. Re-examining the bush on which he had found the message, he said:

"I shouldn't have removed it. You fellows would have been able to figure out whether or not it was put there on purpose. But I'll tell you one thing. My mind keeps going back to those men we saw last night. The shorter chap who went off in this direction could have left this message. And if he's Willie the Penman, the best thing for us to do is to clear out of here. I don't want you boys exposed to any danger on my account."

With one accord, the brothers dismissed this idea.

"You don't think we'd quit now, do you?" Joe demanded. "This trek is too interesting and ex-citing. No, sir, we're staying with you."

"Unless," Frank added, with a wink at Joe, "*you* want to quit, Cap."

"What! And not find the fossil?"

"If Joe and I quit," Frank went on, "we'll have

to give up helping Dad and just when it looks as if Wildcat Swamp may hold a good clue."

"Thanks, boys," the coach said. "But please watch your step more carefully than ever now."

They promised, and Frank added, "Let's keep our eyes open to see if anyone comes for this message."

Although they ate a cold supper rather than signify their presence by the light and smoke of a campfire, no one arrived to pick up the coded note, and finally all three turned in for a good night's sleep. In the morning, the ride toward Wildcat Swamp was resumed with renewed zest.

"The next, and last landmark on the map," Cap stated, "is a big needle rock with a balancing boulder on top. It's on a ledge, halfway down from an overhanging cliff to a long, sandy slope that ends in the swamp itself. The fossil should be somewhere in that sandy slope, between the ledge and the swamp."

Leaving the stream, which whirled away in a southwesterly direction while they continued west, the fossil hunters eventually came to the entrance of a long, narrow defile.

"We must be getting close!" Cap said excitedly. "The map shows this gap leads to the ledge, below which the needle rock is located."

He led the way through the narrow passageway,

with Frank following and Joe trailing with the pack mule. Through the twisting rocky ravine the riders filed, until they could see bright sunlight sparkling at the far end.

"Here we are!" Cap exclaimed as he came out of the dark, shadowy defile onto a wide ledge.

A moment later the boys joined the science teacher on the ledge. To their right was a sheer cliff wall rising to a flat, wide plateau.

To their left, the ledge fell away in a sloping, sandy decline, while straight ahead, at a turn in the ledge, stood the towering rocky column upon which a huge, heavy boulder sat balanced as if on a giant's thumb.

"Look at the size of that boulder!" murmured Joe in amazement. "Yet it is so delicately balanced that it looks as if I could push it off with my bare hands!"

"You might be able to at that," Cap agreed as he studied the phenomenon. "I've seldom seen one so beautifully balanced on such a fine point."

"Look at that wooded mountain beyond the swamp," Joe said. "There's a fire tower at the top."

Frank was about to suggest that they dismount and make their way down to the swamp at the base of the slope when Cap raised a hand for silence.

"Listen!"

Above them on the flat plateau sounded a familiar, steady drumming. Hoofbeats!

"Let's go!" Frank cried, pulling hard on his left rein, then spurring his horse back through the defile and up toward the flat ground above.

With Joe and Cap close behind, it was only a matter of minutes before he burst out through the dark ravine to the open terrain.

Just ahead of them was their quarry, a single horse and rider. With a swoop, the trio surrounded him.

"Why, it's a young boy!" Frank said to himself as the lone rider drew rein.

"Hi, there!" he greeted the youngster, who looked to be about fourteen years old and handled a horse as if he had been born to the saddle.

"Hi, yourself," the boy returned. "Who are you?"

Cap Bailey explained that they were scientists, looking for fossils.

"This happens to be my mother's property," stated the youngster. "Who said you could dig here?"

"Oh, then your mother must be Mrs. Sanderson!" Cap recalled the name from his aunt's letter which had given Mrs. Sanderson's approval of the exploration.

"That's right. I'm Harry Sanderson."

Cap introduced himself and the Hardys, and told Harry why they were on the scene. If necessary, he added, they would be willing to pay for the right to hunt fossils.

"Oh, no, you won't have to do that," Harry assured him. "Mr. Alex Bailey, when he first talked to my mother, promised that she would get all the money any fossils might bring."

"We'll go along on the same promise," Cap assured the boy.

"We liked Mr. Bailey," Harry remarked. "He seemed to be a nice man, but a short while after he settled things with my mother, he disappeared. We heard later that he got sick and died."

"We hope to finish the job he started," Cap told him.

Frank and Joe cautiously questioned the lad, asking who lived in the area.

Harry smiled. "Nobody but us, only lately I've seen campfires and strange men once in a while. The other night a couple of 'em stopped me and started asking a lot of questions. But I slapped my horse and got away. They chased me but couldn't catch me."

"What did the men look like?" Joe asked.

"Both of 'em were big, but one was the biggest man I ever saw! Bet he could be a wrestler if he wanted to. The other man looked like he might be a lawyer or a doctor. He talked in a low voice."

Frank and Joe looked at each other. Without saying a word that might disturb Harry, each knew what the other was thinking. The descriptions fitted Turk and Flint!

CHAPTER VIII

The Treacherous Swamp

"EVEN if those big hombres stop me again," Harry said stoutly, "I'm not afraid of 'em. But if they try anything, I'll get the Forest Rangers after 'em."

"Oh, there are Forest Rangers in this section?" Joe asked.

"Sure thing. They make regular visits through here, and they always stop at our ranch. Matter of fact, they're due just about now. They haven't been around for quite a while."

"Is that the fire tower they use?" Frank asked, pointing to the top of the mountain rising beyond the swamp.

"No. That old one's been abandoned. There's a new tower you can't see from here."

"That's good to know," Cap commented.

"Yeah, and Sheriff Paul's ranch isn't so far from us, either. He's a good friend of ours, too."

"Say, Harry, you must know this territory pretty well," Frank said. "Are we right in thinking that's Wildcat Swamp down there?" He pointed.

"Wildcat Swamp? Never heard it called that, or any other swamp around here."

"Are you sure?" Cap was plainly upset by this sudden revelation.

"That's Devil's Swamp down there," Harry answered.

Cap and the Hardys looked at one another in dismay. Could they be off the track in spite of the map which they had followed so closely?

"Well, I have to get along home," their young informant announced. "Hope you'll all ride over to our ranch sometime. My mother'd like to meet you."

"How do we get there?" Frank inquired.

Harry pointed in a northwesterly direction. "There's a trail along the left side of that mountain."

He slapped his pinto and was off across the plateau in a cloud of dust.

"So this is Devil's Swamp and not Wildcat Swamp, after all," Joe said in disgust. "We come over a thousand miles by plane and train and—"

"Wait a minute," Cap interrupted. "I'm going to check this map again."

For several minutes he studied the detail in silence, then spurred his horse back along the defile.

Coming out on the rock ledge, he dismounted and once more sat surveying the scene. A smile of understanding slowly broke over his face as the boys joined him.

"This has to be the place," he insisted. "There couldn't be two such spots so much alike. Uncle Alex probably named it Wildcat Swamp on his own, not knowing that the local people called it Devil's Swamp."

"There's one way to make certain," Frank remarked. "That's to find the sign about the twenty wildcat."

"If it's still here," Cap said hopefully. "Anyway, let's pick out a place to make camp. Then we can look around."

After scanning the territory for a good location, they agreed upon a wooded section of the plateau just above the mouth of the defile. All three occupied themselves with unpacking their gear, for the first time setting up their tent, and getting perishable camping equipment and supplies under cover.

Cap and Frank found some suitable stones for a permanent fireplace, and arranged them so that they could lay a small grate across the top. This done, the boys were eager to start their exploration.

"Don't do any wandering around here without wearing your high boots," Cap warned. "No telling what you'll run into down at the swamp."

Frank dug out the three pairs of thick wading

boots which they had purchased in Red Butte and they all donned them, along with sturdy corduroy breeches. Light jackets would suffice, they decided, because the sun was still high in the sky.

Cap, still sure that this was the right spot and eager to see if there were any signs of his Uncle Alex's work, told the boys to go ahead. They pigeon-toed their way down the sandy slope to the edge of the green marsh. Frank, remembering Joe's experience with the quicksand, had brought along a length of strong rope in case either slipped into a bad spot.

"What a mixture of growth!" Joe marveled at the lush, odorous tangle before him. "Practically every one of those low trees in the swamp has sucker vines growing all over it."

"And look at those ferns—did you ever see that kind before?" Frank pointed out an unusual, fan-like specimen of lacy greenery.

Frank led the way into the swamp, keeping to the high hummocks and leaping over the black, watery, evil-looking expanses that spread everywhere.

"Isn't it amazing," observed Joe, as he jumped across a particularly wide stretch of dark water to join his brother on a large grassy knoll, "how we passed through such a barren region only a few miles from here and wind up in a wet, waterlogged spot like this?"

"Cap said that's the way this section of the country is—all extremes," Frank returned. "This swamp of course is a low spot surrounded by hills and the stream we were following drains into it."

Joe interrupted his brother by grabbing his arm. "There it is! The old sign!"

To a shaggy willow tree, almost completely enveloped with vines that grew up its trunk and wound around its branches, was nailed an old, weather-beaten board. With a scramble, the Hardys cleared five feet of muck and landed next to the tree.

"This is it! *'Here lie the bodies of twenty wildcat!'*" Joe read.

Frank was so excited that he failed to notice a rustle in the grass beside them. Both brothers heard the loud *hiss-s-s-s* that followed, and their hearts almost stood still as a deadly snake whipped into a coil not two feet from Frank's right leg.

A second later its tongue quivered in readiness to strike!

The snake cracked its head against Frank's calf, recoiled, and lashed out again, this time for a spot above the knee. But before it struck, Joe came out of his frozen stance, took one jump, and landed with his heavy boots on the snake's back. His feet stomped furiously, while the reptile writhed beneath them. Then, ground into the earth, it lay still.

"Thank goodness for these boots," Frank gasped. "If he'd punctured them—"

"You'd have been poisoned!"

The brothers made sure there were no other poisonous reptiles in their vicinity, as they began the hop-skip return to firm ground. Back on the sandy slope at last, they could see Cap making casual explorations into the soil. His first remark after hearing of Frank's narrow escape was:

"Where were the pistols we bought in Red Butte for just such an emergency?"

The Hardys looked sheepish. "Back in camp, where they weren't doing us a bit of good," Joe admitted.

"From now on," Joe changed the subject, "I can see that we're in for some plain, old-fashioned hard work with pick and shovel."

"Correct," the science teacher agreed.

The trio climbed to their camp site, unpacked digging tools, and then headed back to the spot on the slope which Cap had selected.

Swinging the heavy picks, they soon loosened the top layer of sandy soil. But when they had cleared away the soil they had loosened, the harder work began.

"This is really packed down," Frank grunted as he swung the business end of a pick into hardpan and penetrated only a few inches. "If we do very much of this stuff, we'll have shoulders like that guy Turk!"

They had worked for an hour when Cap unearthed an old tin can. He was about to throw it down the slope when he took a second look and let out a surprised yell.

"Bonny Briar smoking tobacco! That's the kind my uncle used to smoke."

"Then we're working in the right place, that's sure," Frank exulted, and stopped to examine the rusty tin. "Unless," the boy amended, "some other guy around here smokes the same brand."

Cap refused to be talked out of his belief and dug with renewed energy. It was only a few minutes later when Joe's pick suddenly hit into the dirt with an odd ringing sound.

"Ouch!" he howled, wringing his hands as he dropped the wooden handle hurriedly. "I could feel that shock all the way up to my elbows!"

"What did you hit?" Cap queried in surprise.

"I don't know, but it sent a vibration right up the handle of this pick."

More careful this time, Joe probed in the same spot, and gradually scraped dirt away from what appeared to be a sheet of metal.

As he worked, the object emerged as a length of heavy, rusted piping. Finally he uncovered its entire length, and they examined the object curiously.

"How in creation did that get in here?" Frank asked, turning to Cap.

The young man was completely stumped. "Uncle Alex wouldn't have used piping," he mused. "And to the best of his knowledge, there had never been any previous exploration here."

They were still standing in amazed study of their unexpected discovery when high above them they heard a great thud and a rumble. Frank, first to look up the slope, gave a shout.

"The boulder! It's toppled off the column! Here it comes!"

With a roar the great stone gathered momentum, sending smaller stones scurrying to all sides, then hurtling down the incline—straight to where the three visitors were digging!

"Look out!" Joe screamed, jumping as far to one side as he could.

Frank was already in mid-air, leaping to the other side.

With a crash the boulder tore across their excavation, pulling what seemed to be half the hillside with it, and thundered into the swamp with a tremendous splash.

Thankful to be alive, Frank and Joe gazed at each other, then looked for their companion.

But Cap Bailey was nowhere in sight!

CHAPTER IX

An Ancient Camel

"CAP! Cap Bailey!"

There was no answer to the boys' frantic calls. Following the thunder of the crashing boulder, the stillness was frightening.

"Quick! We'd better clear away some of this rubble!" Frank ordered.

Rocks and shale of all sizes and shapes had broken loose in the landslide. Sand had been scooped from one spot and piled high in another. Desperately the brothers rooted through the debris.

"Joe! It can't be! Cap just couldn't be—"

"Frank! I see something down there! Khaki, and it's moving!"

The two boys tore wildly at the rubble until they had cleared Cap's face and shoulders. Groggy, the teacher drew in great lungfuls of air, while they continued to pull smaller rocks and sand from the place where he lay half buried.

Finally, he was able to sit up and move his arms and legs to show that he was miraculously unharmed.

"Boulder . . . must . . . have . . . been tipped," he said huskily. "Go . . . see . . ."

Frank and Joe rushed up the slope but could find no trace of any person on the ledge. A quick glance revealed no one near the rock column from which the boulder had become dislodged.

"Let's take a look on the plateau," Joe said, and they hurried along through the defile.

Atop the flat ground, they saw nothing at first that could be connected with the fall of the boulder. Then off toward the trail around the left side of the mountain, Frank's keen eyes spotted a cloud of dust.

"Two riders!" he shouted.

Running to their horses, the brothers flung saddles on them, mounted, and set off in pursuit.

But in less than half a mile, the Hardys knew they could not hope to overtake the fugitives. They had too much of a head start.

"We've got to get back to Cap," said Joe, suddenly remembering the condition in which they had left their companion.

But even from the rock ledge above, the boys could see that Cap looked considerably better. In fact, as they skidded down the incline toward him, he gestured excitedly.

"Look at this!" he exclaimed, and pointed to a

large, odd-shaped object he had picked out of the debris.

Frank and Joe examined it curiously. "What is it?" Frank asked.

Cap looked at them triumphantly. "Unless I'm very much mistaken, this is a bone from the leg of an ancient horse. It was turned up by the boulder when it ripped down the hill."

"An ancient horse? You mean that there were horses in this country so long ago that there are now fossils of them?" Joe asked.

"I thought the horse was a comparatively recent animal—at least, I didn't think they lived in the same age with dinosaurs and flying reptiles," Frank chimed in.

"Oh, no, the horse has been part of the earth as far back as man can tell. As a matter of fact, the evolution of the horse is one of the interesting mysteries of paleontology."

"What do you mean, a mystery?"

"No one has figured out why the horse—a much smaller one than the kind we know today—lived here from prehistoric time until the Pleistocene period, then became extinct. The horse as we know it today was imported."

"But this fossil is from one of the earlier breed?" Frank questioned. "It must be a mighty valuable one, then."

Bailey nodded. "If I'm right, it could mean there

may be many valuable fossils here besides the prehistoric camel my uncle discovered."

Cap was so excited that all thoughts of his brush with death now were forgotten. His discovery seemed to have given him new energy. When the boys told him of the two riders they had chased in vain, he merely nodded.

"If they did tip the boulder, actually they did us a great favor. Look at the digging they saved us."

Frank and Joe were realistic enough to know they had better treat the presence of their enemies with greater respect.

"If they continue to make attempts on our lives," Frank observed, "it just means we'll have to be on guard every second."

"Is there any possibility of getting help in this excavation job?" asked Joe.

Cap shook his head impatiently. Elated by the discovery of the fossil, he was ready to start work immediately.

"If those men were trying to stop us by toppling the boulder, they probably think we're dead, and won't be coming back," he argued. "We can work until dark, and then rig up lights and keep going all night. We've got to get this job finished!"

There was no restraining the scientist. So Frank and Joe, eager themselves to see what other fossils might be turned up, fell to the pick-and-shovel work in earnest.

For several hours they sweated as they got deeper in the sand and hardpan. Once Joe unearthed part of an old shovel, broken and rusted, which Cap thought must have belonged to his uncle.

Later, Frank made a find. He was scraping away some dirt he had already loosened with his pick, when the shovel grated along a comparatively smooth surface.

"Maybe I'm coming to something!" he called out, and the others rushed over to watch as he dug around the object.

When it was uncovered, Bailey was enthusiastic. He examined it carefully, and after much study, turned to the Hardys with a satisfied smile.

"Boys, I think we're catching up with Uncle Alex's work at last. I would bet my last shirt that this bone was once part of the shoulder structure of the ancient camel he thought he'd found."

"Looks to me like an oversize ham bone that some prehistoric dog buried here," was Joe's interpretation of the discovery. He sat down in the sand and propped his weary head on one grimy fist. "You really have to be interested in fossils to work this hard," he groaned. "I'll never think of geologists and scientists again as old fuddy-duddies."

Cap and Frank burst into roars of laughter.

"Better buck up, Joe, we've barely started." Cap clapped him on the back. "You're not going to fall behind an old fuddy-duddy like me, are you?"

"Oh, I didn't mean you, Cap." Joe grinned as he surveyed the trim, youthful figure of his track coach. "I just meant I used to think of scientists as old, stoop-shouldered characters with beards—the way they always look in the comics."

Cap asked Joe to help him carry the ancient bones up to their permanent camp. It required considerable effort in the slippery sand and through the defile, but they finally made it, and laid the fossils under a protective tarpaulin.

"What are we bothering to cover these things for, anyway?" Joe queried. "Nobody's been taking very good care of them for a couple of million years."

"Except Nature," Cap said. "She's been protecting them from the weather all this time."

Looking at the bones, Joe suddenly realized that they might be missing a bet.

"Say, we didn't ever follow the trail of that boulder all the way to the bottom of the slope," he reminded Cap. "It could have turned up something else valuable as it dug a big furrow down the slope."

Cap agreed. "It's worth a try. Let's take a look."

They searched carefully along the excavation which the boulder had made in the sand and shale but found nothing.

"Well, it was a good idea, but I guess the old horse and the ham bone are the only free fossils we'll get this trip!" Joe admitted ruefully while they rested from their efforts.

Back into the pit they went. Frank picked up his shovel again and surveyed the extent of their work.

"Too bad we didn't get this much digging done back on Chet's farm." He grinned. "That bog there would be all cleaned out and Chet could be floating around in his swimming pool by this time!"

"Floating is right!" Cap sighed. "If he is, though, I envy him. I wonder what our well-nourished friend *is* doing right now?"

"Probably stuffing himself with candy, or cookies, or ice cream," Joe answered. "And pretty soon I'm going to start doing something like that. Anyone else hungry?"

Everyone was, so time was called and they proceeded to have some cold beans and dried apricots. Then, refreshed, they vigorously renewed their attack on the slope, determined to uncloak whatever new secrets the earth's treasure chest might contain.

Joe became a little too strenuous in his excavating. Swinging a pick with all his might against a particularly hard surface, he felt the iron snap and found himself with only half a pickax.

"There are a couple of spares up in camp," Cap said, and Joe climbed the slope to replace the broken tool.

Frank and Cap returned to work, chopping out large chunks of near-petrified sand, and the pit grew deeper and deeper. They were working in silence, intent upon the task at hand, when Frank began to feel uneasy.

Where was Joe? He had been gone much too long for a mere trip to replace his broken pick.

Climbing out of the excavation, Frank's eyes scanned the slope that led toward camp. He could not see his brother.

Worried, Frank hurried toward the plateau. Had something happened to Joe?

CHAPTER X

Broken Contact

SENSING trouble, Cap followed Frank, reaching the camp a few minutes later.

"Joe doesn't answer," Frank said. "And," he added, pointing to the undisturbed assortment of tools they had laid out, "I don't think he ever got this far."

"How about the horses?" Cap asked, and quickly investigated the tiny meadow where they had tethered the animals. However, all three and the pack mule were calmly grazing among the scrubby undergrowth.

"I'll try our distress signal," Frank suggested.

Stepping into a clear spot, where no trees could furnish interference of any kind, he sounded a long, piercing whistle, birdlike in quality and far-reaching in tone. It was the secret whistle he and Joe used when in trouble, and many times it had brought one or the other running to his brother's aid.

"That ought to get some result," Cap thought.

But no answer came, and again Frank sent the shrill, high-pitched call through his pursed lips. Listening intently after it ended, all he and Cap could hear was the breeze as it gently moved a few high leaves above them.

"But what could have happened to Joe?" Cap asked. "If he had met with any sort of trouble, we should have heard some kind of sound."

After discussing the situation pro and con, they decided on a systematic search of every foot of ground between the camp and the slope. They had got as far as the ledge when Cap held up a warning hand.

"Do you hear something?" he asked with an uncertain frown.

For a moment there was only silence. Then, almost as if from under their feet, in the depths of the earth, they heard:

"Fra-a-ank! Fra-a-a-a-nk!"

The voice was so low and indistinct that Frank thought he might have imagined it. But a look at Cap's excited face convinced him that his companion had heard the call too.

Where was it coming from?

After several minutes of frenzied search they had the answer. A flash of light from between two huge rocks just below them at the very edge of the slope caught Frank's eye.

"Down there!" he cried excitedly.

He and Cap bent down and peered into the crevice. This time a light shone squarely in their eyes, and they realized that they were staring into the beam of a flashlight.

"Hey! Come on down!" It was Joe's muffled voice. "It's a cave, and somebody's been here!"

Examining the narrow opening, Frank and Cap realized that a man could easily squeeze through it. Rigging a stout rope around a large boulder as a means of ensuring their exit, they wriggled down the rope and into the passageway. In a minute, Frank stood beside Joe Hardy on the floor of a sizable cavern.

"You're okay? You didn't have an accident?" Frank asked.

"Not exactly," Joe answered. "I did fall off the ledge and roll down here. When I saw this cave, I thought I'd— Hey, what's that?"

Cap, following Frank, had precipitated a landslide, as one of his feet slipped off a projecting rock he had used to brace himself. For several seconds, as dirt and rock tumbled down the hole, they feared it might close the opening. But fortunately, the small landslide ceased as abruptly as it had started.

"We'd better get out—and pronto!" Cap advised.

"But I want to show you something first," Joe said.

He pointed with his flashlight to one of the recesses of the cave. Propped against the sloping wall was a skeleton!

"Nice cave mates you pick for yourself, Joe," his brother remarked. He spoke lightly, but a shiver ran down his back as he gazed at the eye sockets of the skull.

"Listen, fellows, that man probably died from suffocation or starvation in here," Cap said. "I wonder whether he had been living in the cave."

"Anyway, he had plenty of equipment with him," Joe said. "See?" His flashlight picked out a pile of long, rusty iron pipes not far from the skeleton.

"Say, they're the same kind of pipe as the one you found on the slope, Joe!" Frank exclaimed. "This old geezer must have brought them down here for a purpose."

"He probably was a prospector of some kind," Cap decided. "I wonder what he planned to do—drain the swamp?"

"But what for?"

"Maybe he had panned some of the slope, and believed it might be a good prospect for placer mining."

All three joined in rummaging around the cave with their flashlights. As Cap was about to suggest they return to the surface, there was a loud exclamation from Frank.

"Come here, quick!"

Hurrying over, they found him in a dark corner. He had spotted a gleaming new pistol.

"Someone else has been down here, and not long ago," he announced. "There's not a speck of rust on this gun."

Carefully, Frank wrapped a handkerchief around the weapon and picked it up. In the palm of his hand, with three flashlights playing on it, they could clearly see the smudges of someone's hand along the barrel.

"I have powder in my pocket, I think," Joe said. "Let's see what those prints look like."

He dusted the smudges, and Frank examined the clear prints. There was a familiar swirl on one that looked like a thumbprint.

"Doesn't that remind you of the thumbprint of a certain character named Willie the Penman?" Frank asked excitedly.

"It sure does—on the kitchen window of Cap's house," Joe replied.

"If so, what's our next move?" Cap asked.

"To prove our point," Frank replied.

He proposed that they leave the pistol in the cave, on the chance that the owner would return to search for his lost pistol, and they could capture him then.

"We can watch from above," the young sleuth suggested.

"Good idea," Joe said, and Cap agreed.

Making sure they had left no telltale traces of their presence, and spreading the small pile of debris which had collected after Cap's descent, by means of the rope they climbed up through the cleft in the rocks to the ledge above.

All agreed that further digging for fossils must wait upon this new development. There was a good chance that the owner of the pistol had been watching them.

Evening chores were split up among them. Cap hid the precious relics, while Frank prepared supper, and Joe watched the cave entrance from a spot in the shadows.

"We'd better use our bedrolls tonight and stay right here," Cap proposed as they finished eating in Joe's hide-out.

By dusk the three watchers were ensconced in a makeshift shelter. Lying prone, they could see every bit of the slope around the entrance to the cavern. A full moon provided all the illumination needed.

"We'd better agree on shifts," Cap suggested, and it was decided that Frank would have the first watch. Joe would take over at midnight, and Cap at three in the morning.

When Joe's turn came he had considerable trouble keeping awake. Suddenly the loud crack of a dead branch brought him to attention. No one was approaching the rock-lined entrance to the cave, however, and he relaxed. He decided that the noise must have been made by a prowling animal.

There were no disturbances during Cap's watch, and at six o'clock he awoke both his companions.

"I was sure somebody'd come back for that pistol," Joe said, disappointment in his voice. "Well, I'm going down to have another look in the cave."

"I'll go with you."

Frank crossed the slope with his brother and descended to the floor of the cave. A moment later the boys looked at each other with astonishment written on their faces.

"The pistol's gone!" they cried simultaneously.

"But how could anyone have taken it?" Joe demanded. "Not a soul came near the cave."

"Unless," Frank said, "there's another entrance."

It took only five minutes for the boys to prove Frank's suggestion. After probing every niche and cranny of the walls, he found a loose boulder which looked as if it had been set in one corner for a purpose. Moving it a bit, Frank saw daylight.

"Come on," Frank motioned, and the two brothers crawled through.

They found themselves farther along the slope, around the corner from the spot where they had lain watching all night!

"What a couple of duds we turned out to be," Frank said in disgust. "And what a laugh Willie or whoever it was had on us!"

"I wonder if they saw us lying there in wait for them—or him!" Joe pondered.

Replacing the stone that covered the entrance, they called to Cap and showed him the second underground entrance. The teacher's reaction was almost identical with Frank's, and he added:

"This place may be riddled with secret caves—and eventually bullets, if we don't watch out."

Several minutes of conjecture produced one decision—to radio Fenton Hardy and tell him that Willie the Penman might be in the neighborhood of Wildcat Swamp.

Frank unpacked the powerful sending and receiving equipment. They surveyed the terrain for a good working spot.

"Below this mountain ridge, we'll certainly have trouble getting a good signal," he murmured, and decided that the only possible way to make contact would be to use the self-inflatable balloon they had brought to carry the antenna aloft.

Soon the little gas-filled bag was high in the sky, trailing its aerial wires. Frank called the secret signal that the Hardys used for family communication. He was about to give it up as hopeless when suddenly a voice said:

"Fenton Hardy speaking. Come in! Come in!"

Quickly Frank reported that they were well, and then told his father of the latest developments at Wildcat Swamp.

"Will you send prints of Flint, Turk, and Willie to Red Butte as soon as possible?" he requested. "We'll check them with the ones on the pistol we found last night."

His father agreed.

"How about the train robbers?" Frank asked. "Any news?"

"I have a hot lead I'd like you boys to—"

Suddenly Mr. Hardy's voice faded completely. There was not a sound from the receiver.

Startled, Frank cast an astonished glance toward the air-borne antenna, just in time to see the balloon, deflated, plummet to the earth.

Now there was no chance to find out what the detective had intended to say.

CHAPTER XI

Ordered to Leave

"WHAT happened?"

Cap's cry was hardly out of his mouth when Joe and Frank were racing off to retrieve the deflated bag. It dropped out of sight, but by following the dual cord which had secured it to the set and carried the antenna line, they soon located it. The balloon hung limply from the branches of a tall pine. Frank shinned up, unfastened the bag, and brought it below for examination.

"Punctured," he said. "Look at those holes." Cap came running up in time to hear the remark.

"But how—so high up in the air? Nobody could throw a stone that far, possibly—not even a baseball pitcher!"

Frank's face was grave. "I believe someone fired a bullet through it."

"But I didn't hear any shot," Joe objected. "Did either of you?"

"The shot could have been fired from the other side of the ridge," Frank commented.

Cap nodded. "Especially if the wind were blowing the other way—and it is—we wouldn't have heard the shot."

"I wonder," Frank mused, "whether some cowboy took a pot shot at it just for fun, or if our friend Willie did it deliberately."

"I wish we could find out just what is behind all these goings on," Cap said. "It doesn't seem likely that a gang of ex-convicts would be worried about our finding a few fossils. What can be the real secret of Wildcat Swamp?"

"It must be important enough for somebody to go to great lengths to protect!" Frank stated with a tight smile.

Slowly, they walked back toward camp, winding the antenna wires on the spindle as they went along. Even though the balloon itself could never again be used, the aerial could be salvaged, and the Hardys had been taught from early youth that waste could be disastrous.

They had almost reached the tent when there came the sound of hoofbeats from behind them, coming down the ravine. Tight-lipped, they waited for the horsemen to appear.

"Oh, it must be the Forest Rangers," Joe announced, relaxing as three green-uniformed men appeared.

The party from Bayport stepped forward to greet the newcomers cordially. But their reception by the rangers was brusque.

"Who are you birds?" one of the rangers asked.

"What are you doing around these parts?" another spoke up.

Courteously, Cap introduced himself and the Hardys, explaining their business in the community.

The leader of the rangers, a short, gruff individual who apparently was indifferent to the fit and condition of his uniform, nodded.

"So I heard," he said shortly. "Well, I have bad news for you. You're going to have to call it all off."

"What do you mean?" Cap demanded.

"I mean that we're ordering you to pack up your stuff and clear out of this territory."

"But we have permission from the owner!" Joe cried belligerently, stepping forward. "She knows all about this expedition!"

"I said you'll have to pack up and clear out," the spokesman retorted in a rasping voice. "If you must know, this is an order from the government."

"For us to get out?" Cap asked unbelievingly.

"Everyone around here has been ordered to move all belongings away," the ranger continued. "It's going to become a government reserve." He backed up his remark by pulling a letter postmarked Washington from his pocket and showing it.

In dismay, Cap and the Hardy boys looked at one another. If the government had closed the territory.

there was no alternative for them but to leave. Cap begged for an extension of time, but was turned down cold.

"Get on the trail!" the ranger ordered.

He and the other men followed the fossil hunters to their camp and stood by to see that they packed up. Discouraged, the three went through the process of folding the tent and dismantling all their permanent fixtures.

"Get a move on! We haven't got all day!" the leader of the rangers commanded, watching the proceedings with a grim smile.

"All right, but we have to pack some of this stuff carefully," Frank answered as he began to stow away the radio equipment.

"Say, son, have you got a state license for that?" the officer asked. "If you haven't we'll just have to take it."

Frank was astounded. "State license? I never heard of such a thing."

"Well, you need it around here," the stocky little spokesman announced. "Short wave, ain't it? Yep, that's the story. Pick it up, men," he ordered the other rangers.

"But you can't do that!" Joe sputtered. "The radio belongs to us."

"Sure, sure, and you can have it back," the ranger said, "by calling at our district office for it next month."

Despite more protests, the rangers, fingering their

holsters, coolly appropriated the set. It was a discouraged, quiet trio which rode off toward Red Butte, with the three men in uniform following them to see that they left the sector as ordered.

Cap was downhearted because he had come so close to finishing his uncle's task. Although he had the two pieces of fossil carefully stowed aboard the pack mule, he was sure other parts of the ancient camel remained on the slope. What a thrill it would have been to find the whole skeleton!

"All right now, just keep going a good ten miles before you stop," called the leader of the rangers. "And after this, do your fossil digging some place else besides Wildcat Swamp!"

There were no words spoken among the three travelers as they jogged along. But as soon as they had put sufficient distance between themselves and the rangers, they halted and held a council of war. It was decided not to put more than a mile between their new camp and the swamp.

"I'm not going to leave here until this whole mystery is solved," Frank said determinedly. "Government reserve or not, if Willie and Turk and Flint have anything to do with this place, I'm going to find out about it."

"Me, too," Joe said. "I never thought of it, but we probably should have told the rangers our suspicions."

"After we compare the fingerprints from the

pistol with those your father's sending," Cap spoke up, "we'll have more to go on."

They dropped off the trail and dismounted near a small brook. Doggedly, they went about the business of establishing their new base in a well-concealed spot.

"Dad said he's sent the prints by air mail," Frank commented. "They'll probably be in Red Butte before we can get there ourselves."

Cap looked at the two brothers more spiritedly than any time since they had been ordered away from the region of the swamp.

"Say, it might be a good idea if I started tonight for Red Butte," he offered. "Then I'd get there just about in time to pick up the letter, and could head back here as soon as I had it. Traveling by moonlight ought to be safer than in broad daylight, the way things are going."

Much as they disliked seeing Cap go off alone, the boys had to agree that his idea made sense.

"In the meantime, we can guard the gear and keep our eyes open for those jailbirds," Frank said.

After a quick supper they helped Cap saddle up, and made sure he had enough provisions to last the trip. After he had ridden off, the boys, deciding against a campfire, crawled into their sleeping bags and lay down.

"I certainly didn't think much of those rangers," Joe remarked with a yawn. "I always thought that rangers were well uniformed, neat, and trim. That little mangy guy was the sloppiest-looking officer I ever saw."

"Say, I've been thinking about that very thing," Frank retorted. "A lot of things those rangers said just didn't ring true—like that license business about the radio."

"They sure were nasty and I've always heard that rangers are polite," Joe said, recalling particularly their leader's parting shot. " 'Do your fossil digging some place else besides Wildcat Swamp,' " the boy repeated in a voice imitating that of the ranger.

Frank suddenly sat up. "Joe! Do you realize what that ranger said? *Wildcat Swamp!*"

"Sure. What about it?"

"Don't you remember Harry Sanderson telling us it's called Devil's Swamp?"

Joe's eyes grew round as he realized the implication. "No local ranger would have called it Wildcat Swamp."

"Exactly. I believe those men were phonies. Let's get back to the slope and see what's going on!"

Quietly, they rode through the brush, keeping off the trail as much as possible, until they were less than half a mile from the upper mouth of the defile. There they tied their horses, and went on afoot.

Down the defile they crept, listening for alien sounds. In a short time they were standing on the rock ledge above the slope. The moon had been blotted out by a cloud a moment before, so now there was blackness all around them.

Joe grabbed Frank's arm. "Look down there!"

Shining from the entrance to the cave was a bright light!

CHAPTER XII

Lost!

"LET's crawl down and look in the cave!" Joe whispered.

"Okay. But take it easy. There may be a guard, and when that cloud passes over, we'll be good targets for him."

Stealthily the brothers crept down the incline. It was treacherous going in the darkness, without the rope, and complete quiet was absolutely necessary.

"Can you see anything?" Joe whispered as they finally reached the lip of the opening and Frank peered cautiously over it.

The answer was a tightening of Frank's grip on his arm. Wriggling closer, Joe's eyes searched downward into the cavern, and he nearly cried out.

Below them were the three rangers!

The Hardys could hear the murmur of their voices but could not make out their muffled words.

Unable to determine exactly what the men were

doing, Joe tried to squirm around for a better view.

On the very edge of the opening, his elbow slipped. Before he could prevent it, a stream of pebbles and stones cascaded down into the cave!

"What's that?" grunted one of the men.

The boys could hear the startled exclamation as the rangers in the cave jumped to their feet.

"Someone's up there! Get 'em!"

Furious that they had been discovered, the two boys jumped to their feet and scrambled up the slope. There was no use trying to be quiet now, and they slipped and stumbled as fast as they could toward the ledge.

Behind them, they could hear the uproar as the rangers gave chase. Just then the moon came out from behind a dark cloud and the ledge was bathed in moonlight.

"Run faster!" urged Frank as they made the ledge and headed for the shadows of the defile.

There was hardly need for Frank's advice. Joe already was tearing along as fast as he could. Just as they reached the entrance to the rocky passageway there was a loud report behind them.

Pt-s-s-s-s-ee-ee!

A bullet whistled overhead, then another, and another. The sound of flying lead lent wings to the feet of the Hardy boys.

"Stay off the trail! Cut across the other way!" muttered Frank.

Joe let his brother pass him. Frank dashed through a tangle of underbrush, up the steep slope of the defile, and into the woods. They struggled over rough ground, running into low-hanging branches, tripping over roots, falling to hands and knees innumerable times.

There was a wild search made with flashlights by the rangers behind them. Again and again the boys dodged the beams. Finally they were able to throw off their pursuers, and they breathed a sigh of relief when all sounds of the chase ceased.

Frank and Joe stopped to rest. After a breathless moment, Joe found his voice to express new concern.

"What if they find our horses!"

"Just hope that they don't. Anyway, we're safe! I wonder where we are. I've lost my bearings completely."

For some time they searched in vain in the darkness for a familiar landmark, but in the shadowy woods there was little they could see. Joe was about to suggest that they give up looking for camp until morning, when Frank said:

"*SSS-s-st!* A light!"

Up ahead, they could see a dim light bobbing in mid-air, as if it were suspended from nothing.

A few seconds later there came the soft clop-clop of a horse's hoofs slowly picking a path among the trees.

"Maybe the rider's meeting someone here," Joe ventured.

Quickly the Hardys found cover, and waited. Within minutes the rider came abreast of their hiding place. The soft glow of the lantern he held lit up his youthful features.

Harry Sanderson!

"Golly, are we glad to see you!" Joe greeted him. "We're lost."

"I'm just as glad to see you!" the boy replied. "I was on my way to find you."

Briefly, Frank explained what had happened, from the time they had been ordered out of the fossil area to the present moment. When he heard their description of the rangers, Harry said they must be new ones. He did not know these men, and oddly enough he had never seen the cave.

"You didn't tell us Wildcat Swamp was to become a government reserve," Joe chided him.

Harry's eyes flicked wide open in amazement. "It's not true. I mean, my mother and I haven't heard anything about it."

"You haven't? The Forest Ranger had a letter telling about it."

"What! It looks more and more as if something mighty funny's going on. A man came to our ranch this evening to buy it for himself."

Harry went on to say that a stranger had dropped in with papers to show his mother that Devil's Swamp and a lot of the ranch really belonged to someone else, and the man was going to buy it from the real owner.

Frank and Joe were baffled by Harry's revelations. They began to realize that a great deal was happening in the Wildcat Swamp neighborhood that was mysterious and which their father would want them to investigate.

"All my mother really owns," Harry went on, "is the house and a few acres around it—at least that's what the man said. When she cried, he told her, 'Don't worry. The swamp ain't worth anything, anyhow!'"

"Who was this man?" Frank asked, his eyes flashing with indignation.

"His name was George Moffet. I never saw him before. Guess he doesn't live around here. He was a little guy, pale and beady-eyed."

"Willie the Penman, I'll bet!" Joe exclaimed.

"Willie who?" Harry asked.

Without telling him that Willie was an ex-convict, Joe said he had acquired the name because he could imitate other people's signatures.

"If your caller was Willie, he probably wrote the papers himself," Frank said. "Harry, you tell your mother not to give up any papers and not to sign any unless we see them first. She shouldn't even show her deed to the land to this imposter. Keep it locked up in a safe place. Hurry!"

"Thanks a lot, fellows," Harry said. "I knew you'd help me. But before I go, I want to help you. I'll take you to your horses."

The boy, familiar with every section of the Sanderson ranch, led the Hardys toward the spot where they had tied their horses. A short distance from the place they told Harry to wait, and crept forward. Both animals were safe. Apparently the rangers had departed.

Leading their mounts to where Harry was waiting with his horse, they said good-by, leaped into their saddles, and reached the camp without further adventure.

To their relief, nothing had been disturbed, and once more they crawled into their bedrolls. Next morning the brothers discussed the strange events of the previous evening.

"Doesn't it strike you as strange that three new rangers were sent here in addition to the others already located in this area?"

Frank nodded. "And it's not natural for men in that position to be whispering in a cave. I'd like to sneak back to the swamp in daylight and see what's going on."

"Go ahead. I'll watch camp. We can't take a chance on having our stuff stolen."

As soon as they had eaten, Frank went off to reconnoiter. His careful approach through the defile and the ledge was effort wasted, he discovered. There appeared to be no one anywhere around, and no trace whatever of the men who had been there only a few hours before.

Without Joe to stand guard for him outside, Frank did not attempt to enter the cave, but he did play his flashlight into both entrances and satisfied himself that they were vacant. The only explanation he could think of was that the rangers might comprise a special group to evacuate people from the new government reserve. If the Sanderson ranch actually was to be turned into a reserve!

Back at camp, he said to Joe:

"As soon as Cap gets back I think we can take a chance digging again. As long as we don't carry away any fossils, there won't be any harm in looking for them."

Joe agreed. In the meantime, he wanted to keep busy.

"I think one of us had better get in touch with Mrs. Sanderson," he said. "Harry may have been stopped before reaching home."

"I'll stand guard here this time," Frank offered. "You ride over to the ranch."

With Harry's directions to guide him Joe started out for the Sanderson ranch house. The path led over fairly rough country on the other side of Wildcat Swamp. Joe saw no evidence of grazing cattle, though there were occasional grassy stretches that would have afforded pasturage. He scared up several rabbits, and even took a pot shot at a fox about to devour one.

Presently the way led up through another rocky

defile, similar to the one near camp. Joe was halfway through this narrow ravine when he heard the sound of horse's hoofs from up ahead. The horseman was coming straight in his direction and there was no place around in which the boy might hide from a possible enemy.

The strange rider bore down on him from around a curve in the trail. Suddenly, twenty paces ahead, the newcomer's horse shied, stumbled over a loose stone, and threw his rider headlong.

Like a sack of meal, the rider struck the ground, and lay still.

"This can't be a trick," Joe thought to himself. "He hit the earth too hard!"

Cautiously, nonetheless, Joe dismounted and approached the fallen rider, who had not moved.

Joe took hold of him, turning the rider over on his back.

It was Chet Morton!

CHAPTER XIII

Three Odd Letters

"CHET! Chet Morton!" Joe shouted in disbelief.

His friend did not stir. Joe flipped the top off his canteen and held the cool water to Chet's lips. The boy moaned and tried to rise. Finally he succeeded in propping his head on one elbow.

"Joe! No, it couldn't be. I guess I'm dreaming. I'm still kayoed."

"You're not dreaming, Chet. What are you doing 'way out here?"

The stout boy rested several seconds before replying.

"Morton's Pony Express. Modern variety," he answered cheerfully. "Boy, that spill knocked the wind out of me. I have a message for you guys. Several, in fact."

"Is Dad okay?" Joe asked apprehensively. "And the family?"

"Oh, sure. Your dad and I flew to Red Butte together yesterday afternoon with Jack Wayne."

"You and Dad?"

"Yeah. He's hot on the trail, I guess. Those train robbers are going to take the choo-choo to the hoose-gow."

"Well, what's the news?" Joe asked eagerly.

"I have the fingerprint pictures you asked for," Chet said as he struggled awkwardly into his saddle.

Anxious to be on his way to the Sanderson ranch house, Joe tried to tell his friend where camp was located. But Chet looked baffled. Finally, Joe climbed into his own saddle. "Come on, Chet," he said. "I'll show you the way back to camp and while I'm there I'll compare those prints with the ones we found on the pistol."

As they rode along, Chet told Joe the reason for his sudden trip to the West.

"Your dad thought I'd enjoy it," he began. "And also, he didn't trust anyone else to bring a certain message. He thought Sheriff Paul probably would know where you were, so just before he took the midnight train, he told me to contact the sheriff and have him take me to Wildcat Swamp."

"Where did Dad go?"

"He was very secretive as usual," Chet said with a grin.

"Did Sheriff Paul bring you?"

"No, he wasn't at his office," Chet replied. "Girl

there told me he was ill, so I rode out to his ranch. But he wasn't there. Nobody was."

"Then how did you find this place?" Joe asked.

"A nice kid reined up in front of the Paul ranch house just as I was about to leave," Chet said. "Name of Harry Sanderson."

"We know him."

"Yeah, he told me you did, and he showed me how to get here. He led the way for a while. Knows all the short cuts. And boy, he can ride like the wind!"

Chet paused for breath, then asked, "How's Cap?"

"All right, I hope. He went to Red Butte. Funny you didn't see him at the hotel."

"He wasn't registered."

This turn of events worried Joe. Had Bailey been attacked on the way to town?

"Nothing seems to be turning out right on this expedition," he told Chet, and brought him up to date on all that had happened.

"At least you now have a copy of the fingerprints you wanted," Chet remarked with pride.

Arriving at camp, Joe flung himself from the saddle. "Hi, Frank!" he yelled. "Look what I found along the trail."

"Chet! How'd you get here? You look as if you'd ridden all the way from Bayport."

"I had a spill," Chet confessed. Then, repeating

his mission, he pulled a packet from his jeans and handed it to Frank.

Eagerly Frank tore it open. It contained magnified copies of three sets of fingerprints—Turk's, Willie's, and Gerald Flint's. The Hardys at once compared them with the prints taken from the pistol.

"Look at this whorl," Joe cried excitedly. "No mistaking it. As sure as shooting the gun we found in the cave was once in the hands of Willie the Penman. And I'll bet it is in his shoulder holster right now!"

Chet let out a whistle. "He's—he's after you guys?"

"Guess he is," Frank said.

"In that case"—Chet gulped—"I'd better get back to Bayport and finish digging our swimming pool."

"Before you eat?" Joe needled him.

Chet grinned. "What're you offering?" He walked toward a case of canned food and began inspecting the labels. "I'll stay till morning," he called. "Got to get some rest."

During the evening the boys waited expectantly for Cap's return, hoping someone in Red Butte had told him about Chet's arrival. But Cap did not come.

"I'm afraid he never reached Red Butte," Frank said fearfully. "And now that we know definitely

Willie the Penman is in the neighborhood, I'm worried."

With concern on his face, Chet pulled a bright bandanna from his pocket and mopped his brow. "Honest, fellows, I have to start back for Bayport in the morning. You don't need me here."

"But as long as you are here, wouldn't you like to help us dig up a camel?" Joe suggested.

"A what!"

"That's right. We've found one. Honest."

Chet began to weaken. "Well, I might hang around a day or two."

When morning came and Cap still had not appeared, the Hardys felt that one of them should go to Red Butte to investigate.

"I'll volunteer," Chet offered.

He mounted his horse like a bear cub trying to straddle a split-rail fence.

"Hold it!" Joe said suddenly. "Did you give us all of Dad's messages?"

"Hey, it's good you reminded me," Chet answered. "I forgot something."

"What?"

"Your dad wants to see you."

"When?"

Chet pushed his Stetson back and scratched his head. "Let's see. Just before midnight on the seventeenth, I think it was."

"Where?" Frank asked impatiently.

"On the railroad siding near Spur Gulch." Chet pulled a map from his pocket and handed it over.

"And you almost forgot to tell us!" Joe exploded. "The seventeenth is tomorrow!"

Embarrassed by his lapse of memory, Chet slapped his horse and was off among the trees. He turned once to wave, then rode out of sight.

"Frank, that's real news from Dad," Joe exclaimed. "Something's doing. A trap for the train robbers, or I miss my guess."

"Could be," Frank returned. "I sure hope we can clear up some of the mystery around here before we leave to meet Dad. I think we ought to find Sheriff Paul and tell him about Willie the Penman. And we still have to see Mrs. Sanderson."

The brothers decided to set off at once. They would have to risk leaving their camping equipment, which they hid in a rocky depression, covering it with brushwood.

It was quite a long ride to Sheriff Paul's ranch, but they reached it finally. Picketing their horses, they knocked on the back door, which immediately was opened by a trim, middle-aged woman. When the boys introduced themselves, she asked them in.

"We have a few worries we'd like to talk over with the sheriff," Joe said.

"My husband is not here," Mrs. Paul replied. "And I have a few worries too. He hasn't been home for three days."

"Three days? We heard he was home ill," Frank remarked.

"No. He got a phone call and told me there was trouble about some rangers. I didn't get the details, because he rode off in a great hurry."

Joe gave his brother a sidelong look. Rangers! Could it be the same three men who had ordered Frank, Cap, and him away from the swamp? Frank caught his brother's glance and nodded in reply.

"I guess we'd better leave a note for the sheriff," Frank told Mrs. Paul, who promised to give it to him as soon as he returned.

"Maybe we'd better return to where we hid our supplies and not go to the Sanderson ranch just now," Frank told Joe.

The boys left and headed back toward camp. When they were still some distance from it, Frank, hearing voices, reined in suddenly. Dismounting, he and Joe walked forward cautiously.

"Chet! Cap!" Frank cried.

Questions flew in all directions at once. Chet and Cap had met shortly after the stout boy had left for Red Butte. The coach, having heard about Chet's arrival and departure from a restaurant owner, had started back but had lost his way.

"I-I like it better here now," Chet said. "I think I'll stay till you all go. With Cap here, there are four of us. Just let Willie the Pen dare to poke his head in!"

The tension relieved, they all laughed and set about preparing supper. Chet ate until Joe asked him if he thought he was filling up a prehistoric camel.

"There's nothing prehistoric about me!" mumbled Chet, pushing another hot biscuit into his mouth.

As evening fell and there still was no sign of the rangers, Frank said, "Let's sneak back and do some more digging tonight."

Armed with flashlights and tools, the four carefully made their way down to the fossil deposit. Chet was impressed, and wanted to see more of the camel. However, he soon tired of the digging.

"What's the matter, Chet?" Joe asked. "Break your shovel?"

Chet grunted and went to work. It was becoming evident that the fossil they were excavating was an enormous one.

"I believe we have a perfect specimen," Cap said enthusiastically.

Chet found plenty of excuses to rest from his labors. Only the sarcastic remarks of his friends kept him digging in the spot designated to him. He had not been at it long when he unearthed a half-rotted board.

"Huh," he said, "all I can do is find clam fossils in Bayport and old billboards out here."

Frank looked up suddenly. "Billboards? Where?"

"Here," Chet said, beaming his light on the rotten piece of wood. "It has letters on it. E R S. What does that mean?"

"Could be part of the name Sanderson," Joe said.

"Perhaps an old prospector left it here," Cap volunteered.

Frank snapped his fingers. "I have it!" he cried. "Wait here. I'll be back in a second."

Without explaining why, he dashed off in the darkness.

"I think he ate some loco weed," Chet remarked, leaning on his shovel and heaving a sigh.

The words were hardly off his lips when a shriek of terror sounded in the night.

Was Frank in trouble?

CHAPTER XIV

Underground Snare

CATAPULTING himself out of the pit, Joe dashed down the slope in the direction Frank had taken. Chet and Cap hurried after him, despite the treacherous downgrade. With their flashlights stabbing the blackness, they finally reached the edge of the swamp.

Just then a flashlight beam was turned on Joe and a familiar voice called, "What's going on? You guys sound like a stampede of water buffalo."

"Frank! Was that you who yelled?"

"No. I thought it was one of you."

"Must have been a wildcat," Cap ventured. "They sometimes sound like humans."

"Say, Frank, where were you going in such a rush?" Chet asked.

"To get that sign on the tree. I have an idea about it."

With the others following, he pushed through

the dark swamp toward the gnarled willow tree.

"Keep an eye out for snakes this time!" Joe advised.

"Snakes? Are there snakes around here?" Chet inquired in a shaky voice. "This is a fine time to tell me! I'd have stayed back on firm ground."

Joe laughed. "Oh, just little ones, Chet. The critter that tried to take Frank's leg off last time we were down here couldn't have been over six feet long."

There was a low moan from the chubby member of the party, but rather than be left alone in the marsh, Chet kept right on with the others.

When they reached the tree, Frank pointed out the dangling sign to Chet. Then he yanked the weathered old board loose.

"I want to compare this with the piece of wood you found, Chet," he said.

As they struggled back up the hill to the pit, Chet puffed and heaved. "You sure—make things—hard," he said.

Joe was first to notice that something was amiss at the pit.

"Hey! I left my shovel right here. Where'd it go?"

"Everything's gone!" cried Cap.

"The board too," Frank said. "We've been robbed!"

"That cry was just a trick to get us away from here," Cap declared. "Somebody wanted our tools.

Put out your lights, boys. There's no sense making class A targets out of ourselves."

The four stood motionless in the darkness. Frank broke the silence by whispering that it would be hopeless to try finding the thief in the darkness, especially with so much cover for him everywhere. The logical move was to return to their camp site as secretly as possible.

The others had to admit that Frank's suggestion made sense. By this time all of them except Chet knew the route well enough to find it in the dark. Chet stumbled along between Frank and Joe. Reaching camp, they crawled into their sleeping bags, without making a light, and lay down.

"Now tell us about the sign, Frank," Chet whispered.

"I was going to try fitting the two pieces together. I think originally it was all one sign."

"But that would mean it doesn't refer to wildcats at all," Chet pointed out.

"Right! It would read, 'Here lie the bodies of twenty wildcatters!' "

"Wildcatters has two Ts," Joe reminded him.

"The second T could have been right on the break," Frank explained, "and easily have rotted away."

Chet still did not see the real significance. "What's the difference whether there were twenty wildcats or twenty wildcat hunters here?"

This time Cap spoke up. "Frank has made an excellent deduction. A wildcatter, Chet, isn't an animal hunter. He's a man who hunts for oil well locations."

"Oil prospectors!" Chet whistled. "You mean there might be oil here?"

Cap said that was quite possible, and then Joe exclaimed, "Those rusty pipes we found could have been part of some drilling equipment! And that skeleton in the cave might have been another one of the wildcatters!"

"Sk-skeleton!" Chet quavered.

"Oh, we didn't tell you about our Mr. Bones!" Joe laughed. "Wait till you see him. He's out of this world."

Chet crawled deeper into his sleeping bag and was silent.

"Seriously," Frank said a moment later, "I wonder what really happened to those wildcatters, and when?"

"I've been mulling that over myself," came Cap's voice, "and I've about decided that it couldn't have been too long ago."

"I think you're right," said Frank.

"Well, I feel we can be certain," Cap said, "that there still may be a few men living who learned about the possibility of oil being below the swamp from some of those wildcatters. That's why they're trying to run us out of here."

Frank remarked that a certain George Moffet, real name or not, seemed to fit right into this theory. No doubt he was trying to get Mrs. Sanderson's property away from her.

"Is there any way of telling where there might be oil except by drilling?" Chet asked Cap.

"Yes, indeed," the teacher replied. "In certain periods in prehistoric times far more oil deposits were formed than in others. If I could locate some fossils from one of those periods, I'd know we've made the right guess about the situation here. Incidentally, every big oil company today employs a paleontologist for this kind of exploration."

"If we're going to do any more digging," Chet spoke up, "we'll have to buy some more tools."

"Joe and I might get them in Red Butte after we see Dad," Frank suggested. "Tomorrow night we plan to meet him at Spur Gulch, Cap," he added, and told him about the message Chet had brought.

Bailey volunteered that he and Chet buy the tools. They would stop at the Sanderson ranch and tell Harry and his mother their suspicions.

Next morning, an hour after sunup, Frank and Joe set off in an easterly direction, while the others went northwest.

"I'd like to look around that cave once more before we leave," Cap said when they reached the ledge. "Besides examining those pipes again, we may find other clues to prove we're on the trail of the old wildcatters or of some new ones."

Chet was reluctant. He had no desire to see the skeleton, but on the other hand, he didn't want the teacher to think he lacked courage. At last he said:

"Okay, Cap. Lead the way!"

When they reached the narrow opening in the rocks, Chet glibly offered to remain at the cave entrance "to guard the horses." Cap grinned as he dismounted.

"If there's trouble," the teacher said, "we're better off together than split up."

"You've talked me into it," Chet replied solemnly.

Flashlight in hand, Cap stalked ahead of him down the incline to the cave entrance below the ledge. At the end of the passage, where it broadened out into the wider portion of the cave, Bailey's light flickered.

"Battery's getting low," he muttered to himself.

As Chet beamed his own light around, Cap entered the inner part of the cave. Stepping past the skeleton, barely discernible in the dim light, the teacher bent to pick up a rusted section of pipe. As he did, a faint sound in a recess of the rock wall made him straighten up.

"That you, Chet?"

"What did you say?" Chet boomed from the passageway.

In sudden alarm, Bailey swung his fading flashlight toward the wall. It picked up a dark figure crouching in the gloom.

"Don't move!" came a whispered command.

At the same moment, an arm behind him snaked around his chest like a hoop of iron, pinioning his own arms to his sides. With a clatter, Cap's flashlight dropped to the rock floor.

"Chet!" he gasped. "Get help! Hurry!"

"Shut up!" his attacker hissed.

The arm tightened its grip, choking off any further warning. As Cap struggled, the other man leaped from his corner and rapped him sharply on the side of the head with the butt end of his gun. The science teacher crumpled to the floor.

"That'll take care of him for a while!" the gruff voice muttered in the darkness. "Now let's get the other one."

"I hope he didn't hear the warning," his helper whispered.

But Chet, having heard Cap's desperate plea for help, stood wondering what to do. Should he run for help, or go to the teacher's assistance?

And where could he go for aid? Frank and Joe were too far away to be overtaken. The Sanderson ranch and the sheriff's home were out of the question.

At this moment Chet heard a man's voice. He made his decision. Even though he was scared, Chet was not the kind of person to run out on a friend in distress.

"If someone's hurt Cap," he said to himself, "I'll—I'll—"

Chet once had learned some elementary judo. Ready for whatever lay ahead, he went onto the attack, moving forward watchfully. Whoever was in the cave would be coming for him any moment, he felt sure. As a flashlight suddenly beamed in the passageway, Chet poised himself. Seconds later a burly-looking man emerged from the inner room.

As Chet had been taught, he let out a blood-curdling scream and shouted some unintelligible gibberish. His amazed adversary stopped in his tracks. The boy backed away a few inches. If he could keep this up until he reached the entrance—

The man, though, was not to be fooled a second time. He lunged savagely at the boy. Instantly Chet grabbed his outstretched arms and pulled his attacker sharply forward. Off balance, the man stumbled toward him.

With split-second timing, Chet brought his knee up sharply against the man's chin. He went down like a sack of lead sinkers.

Not knowing there was a second enemy, Chet relaxed. Suddenly his hands were locked behind him in a firm grip. He tried to break free, but this new foe twisted the boy's arms painfully.

Resistance was impossible.

CHAPTER XV

Ambush

WHILE Chet struggled against his new enemy, the man he had knocked down began slowly to get to his feet. Holding his jaw, he shone a big flashlight on the boy and glowered.

"Wise guy, eh? Break his arm, boss."

"Can the cracks!" came the terse reply. "Get on with this job!"

The injured man's companion snapped handcuffs on Chet's wrists. The boy was shoved deeper into the cavern, where the big fellow stuck a candle into a crevice and lighted it.

In the eerie glow Chet saw Cap lying prone on the ground. Then, for the first time, he got a good look at the second assailant, a small, wiry man wearing a badly fitting green uniform and holding a short rifle.

As Chet stared, Cap came to and staggered to his feet. Shaking his head to clear it, he suddenly recognized their captors.

"You're the rangers who ordered us out of this area!" he charged.

"Very clever!" the scrawny man said sarcastically. "But since you weren't smart enough to take a friendly warning, we're going to teach you a lesson!"

"Listen here," Cap exclaimed angrily, "if you're really rangers, I demand that this boy and I be treated according to law. You have no right to hold us without a valid complaint."

"No? Well, we're takin' the right."

"You can't get away with this!" Chet said hotly. "We know who you are, and we know what you're after! You're impostors, and you're trying to steal Mrs. Sanderson's land!"

"And you," Cap added, pointing at the wiry man, "you're Willie the Penman!"

"Boss," the big man cried, "they know we—"

"Shut up!" the other ordered. He turned to Cap and Chet. "You don't know what you're talking about. If you have any sense at all, you'll keep your mouths shut." He turned back to his companion. "Give me the wire."

The captives were led deeper underground, back into the dim recesses of the cave. Then the men, using lengths of tough copper wire, tied their prisoners' hands behind their backs, and bound their ankles.

"Are we being kidnaped?"

The big man snickered, and the bossy little fellow said with an ugly laugh, "I wouldn't call it that. We're not taking you anywhere. You're just going to lie right here in this cave and have a good rest."

"Yeah, and when we get around to it," his buddy added, "we'll send the sheriff to pick you up."

With that, the two men left the cave. When the sound of their footsteps had died away in the gloomy vault, Chet spoke up. "Do you think they really will send the sheriff to get us?"

"I wouldn't count on it," Cap replied. "I can't picture those two criminals helping the law."

"Do you suppose Frank and Joe will ever find us?" Chet quavered.

Meanwhile, Frank and Joe had altered their plans. Since they did not have to meet their father until midnight, they had decided to ride first to Sheriff Paul's and find out about the "ranger trouble."

Reaching the place and dismounting, the boys knocked on the front door. To their amazement, it swung wide open under Frank's touch.

Joe called out, but there was no reply. He peered into the neat living room.

"The place is deserted! How about that! Even the note we left is still on the table."

"That's funny," Frank remarked. "Mrs. Paul must have gone off soon after we did."

"I hope nothing happened to her," Joe said apprehensively.

The boys circled the house, but there was no sign of the sheriff's wife. Nor was she in the barn or any of the other ranch buildings. The boys were more mystified than ever.

"Let's go into the house," Frank suggested, mounting the back steps.

In the kitchen they saw unwashed dishes on the sink—a startling contrast to the spick-and-span condition of the house. Near the door was a basket of clothes. On a hunch, Frank felt of them.

"They're still damp, Joe. That means Mrs. Paul was interrupted in her work. She must have left here in a hurry. Let's check the corral."

Joe, first to reach it, called out, "Look at these fresh hoofprints. Several riders were here."

Frank knelt down. "Three sets come up to the gate, and then four go away. The question is, did Mrs. Paul go with the others?"

Carefully checking the trail, and the turnoff into the ranch, the boys discovered that one set of hoofprints were headed in another direction, and ventured a guess that Mrs. Paul had left in a hurry, after the three other horsemen had gone.

"She might have ridden off to warn somebody about her visitors," Joe surmised, "probably her husband. But why didn't she use her radiotelephone? I noticed one in the living room."

Hurrying back to the house, Frank examined the set. "The sheriff no doubt uses it to contact police headquarters at Red Butte. I'll do the same."

He switched on the set and waited for it to warm up. However, no answering hum came from the loud-speaker. He pressed the microphone button.

"That's funny, Joe. This set doesn't seem to be putting out at all."

Frank tried again, but the output dial remained at zero. Turning off the set, Joe unsnapped the cover slides, and removed the top.

"No wonder," he exclaimed. "A tube is missing!"

"That's proof enough for me," Frank cried. "Those visitors were here for no good reason."

"We'd better ride to Red Butte as fast as we can and report the whole situation," Frank said grimly.

"Right," Joe agreed. "Then later we might hop a train from there to Spur Gulch."

Hurrying outside, the Hardys sprang into their saddles and galloped off. Soon more than a mile had been covered at the rapid pace. Then they were forced to slow down because the trail had entered a rocky valley.

"This is tough on the horses," Joe remarked.

As they proceeded, the valley became a narrow pass walled in by steep rock formations on either side.

"I guess it'll have to be Indian file now!" Frank

said, cantering in front of his brother. As they neared the end of the pass, he suddenly reined in.

"What's up?" Joe asked, almost colliding with Frank's mount.

Frank did not answer, but from up ahead, Joe could hear a gruff voice shout:

"Hold it!"

A man in rough cowboy attire, astride a pony, blocked the exit to the pass. The boys couldn't see what he looked like, because of a dirty blue kerchief tied over the lower part of his face, and a ten-gallon hat pulled low on his forehead.

"I see you're packing a gun!" he remarked, looking at the weapon Frank carried in a holster.

"Yes. Protection against animals."

"Oh, yeah?"

The cowboy gave a short, nasty laugh. Then he pressed his horse up beside Frank's mount and tried to make a quick grab for the boy's gun.

But Frank, suspicious of the masked stranger, was alert. As the officious rider's arm shot out toward his holster, the boy stood up in his stirrups and brought his fist down hard on the man's wrist.

Frank's gun clattered to the ground. His horse reared, making the stranger's pony shy too, and the masked man lost his seat. His own weapon was dislodged and flew several feet away as he hit the sand.

"Hey, what the—" he shouted.

"Come on, Joe!" Frank cried. "Help me tie this guy up, quick!"

As Joe slid off his mount, he grabbed the rope from the pommel of his saddle and hurried to assist his brother. It was dangerous business, maneuvering in the narrow pass among the excited, rearing animals.

Scrambling to his feet, Frank's assailant began to back out of the pass. He reached for his gun. Realizing it was gone, he turned tail and started to run.

"Help!" he shouted.

Frank and Joe ran to intercept him. Joe tackled the man about the knees and dragged him to the ground. Frank, following up this move as fast as he could, seized the man's flailing arms.

But even as he did, the boy spotted a quick flash of movement to his left.

"Watch out, Joe!" he yelled. "There are more of them!"

Two other masked men who had been crouching at the mouth of the defile, hidden from observation, now sprang forward. As the brothers whirled to meet this new threat, the two ambushers charged!

CHAPTER XVI

An Icy Dungeon

"GET 'em!"

Though completely snowed under by the double-barreled Hardy attack, the mysterious stranger managed to shout orders to his oncoming aides.

Frank side-stepped a fist from one of the other masked men and landed a hard blow on the attacker's chest. As Joe ducked a charge from the third ambusher, their fallen leader arose and dived at the boy from behind.

Thrown off balance, Joe was an easy target for his two opponents, and went down like a tenpin. Against three, Frank stood no chance at all, and was quickly pulled to the ground.

Within a matter of minutes, the brothers were bound and gagged, then heaved crosswise onto the saddles of their horses.

"This must be some of Willie's gang," thought Frank as the horse started to move. "Now what?"

124

There was no indication from the cowboys as to where they were taking the Hardys. Except for a terse command now and then by their leader, the men guided the Hardys silently on a grueling ride through the rough country. Two of their captors rode ahead, the other at the rear.

"Why have they kidnaped us?" Joe's mind was in a whirl. "How did they know where to wait?"

"Who are they?" Frank wondered. "Where are they taking us?"

One hour went by, two, three. Frank and Joe had been in many a tight spot, but none ever had seemed so hopeless as this one. Each jog of horse and saddle against stomach and ribs knocked the breath from their bodies. The boys realized they were becoming so exhausted and sore that, even if they could manage to struggle free, they would not be able to walk.

Worst of all, they realized that they now would have no chance of meeting their father at Spur Gulch.

Hours later Frank and Joe heard the whistle of a train and shortly afterward they were approaching the railroad line. As best Frank could figure, they had traveled due south, then southwest, and they were intersecting the railroad right-of-way much farther west than Spur Gulch.

From behind a massive rock beside the shimmering tracks came the sudden sound of a horse's whinny. The man in the lead halted. He thrust two fingers in his mouth and gave a shrill whistle. Immediately two more masked men rode into view.

"So you got the meddling kids!" one of them boomed. "Great work! We'll get rid of 'em right away!"

"What's your plan?" asked one of the others.

"Toss 'em on the rails!"

From their awkward positions, lying across their saddles, the boys studied the newcomer. He was a big, heavy-set fellow, just as Jesse Turk was supposed to be. Could this be the convict who had so cleverly escaped from Delmore Prison?

The other man shook his head. "I can't go for that method."

"Why not? Let the buzzards destroy the evidence!" He glanced up and gave a short, ugly laugh. "There are a couple of hungry ones up there right now."

"You want us all sent up for life—just when we can get clear?" the other man shot back. "I've got an idea how to put these smart-alecky kids out of the way and make it look like an accident."

"How?"

"The freight that's coming through here from the west at ten-thirty is hauling refrigerator cars. It's due in an hour. We'll put these bozos on ice!"

"Hey, that sounds like a good deal. I'll go for that, myself." And the others readily agreed.

"While we're waiting, how about a little chow?"

one of the men suggested. "I'm so hungry I could eat a horse."

One of the others guffawed. "We'll have two extra nags after the freight goes by!"

Raucous laughter followed this remark, and then the heavy-set fellow spoke up again. "Break out some chow. We'll give these boys their last meal."

As Frank's and Joe's horses were led away from the main party, their guard drew a bowie knife. Dismounting, he slashed the ropes that bound Frank's wrists and ankles.

"Get off and untie your brother," he ordered roughly. "And no tricks! Hear me?"

Frank was only too glad to obey. He unfastened the handkerchief that had been stuffed into his mouth, and hobbled over to where Joe still lay across his mount. While seeming to struggle with his brother's knotted bonds, he whispered furtively:

"Joe, I'm sure two of those men are the ones we captured at Green Sand Lake. Flint and Turk!"

"I think you're right. But we're not going to sit here and let them get away with this, are we?"

"I'll say not! Dad wants these crooks, and we'll get 'em! Soon as we get the kinks out of us, I'll give you the signal and we'll put up a fight."

"Cut it out," the guard shouted. "No talking!"

By the time Joe was untied, their supper was brought to them by another masked man. Seated with a rifle across his knees, he watched the captives eat. The boys were hungry enough for a good meal, even though their minds were occupied by the grave danger facing them.

As Joe set down the tin can from which he had been drinking water, he whispered, "Frank, how come they left only one guard over us? Where are the rest of them?"

Frank smiled grimly. "The others wanted to eat, I guess, and you can't eat with a bandanna over your mouth! They don't want us to see who they are."

Hearing their murmuring, the guard turned. "All right, you wise guys, one last warning. You want your gags back on? One more sound outta you, and—" Suddenly he stopped, cocked his head, and let out a loud roar. "Well, we don't have to worry about you much longer. Here comes the freight."

As the train drew nearer, the rest of the gang appeared and surrounded the captives.

"Get ready for your last mile," cracked the brawny man sardonically. "Curtains for two detectives—and one to go!"

The boys winced. By "one to go" the scoundrel could not mean anyone but their father. They must know he was in the vicinity of Spur Gulch! He might even have been captured already!

Crouching behind a low outcropping of rock along the tracks, the men forced the two boys down with them. The railroad ran up a slight grade at this place, and the heavy Diesels struggled and churned as they reached the incline. Slowly, the twin locomotives neared the hidden group.

"This'll be a snap," one of the men said confidently. "I'll break the seal on a cooler first, and then—"

Suddenly Frank sprang up. "At 'em, Joe!"

"Hey, what's—"

The man's cry was cut off abruptly as Joe's fist crashed into his mouth. Blood spurted from the man's lip, and he gave a yell of surprise and pain.

Shoving one of their abductors backwards into another and sending both sprawling, Frank turned and butted headfirst into a third.

As they battled against the heavy odds, the boys shouted at the top of their voices for help. But their cries were lost in the thunder of the Diesels as the big engines roared past. No one on the train had seen the ruckus, and now no one could hear it!

Although the Hardys fought furiously, they couldn't handle such overwhelming odds. Subdued, they were held this time in steellike grips. The man who had proposed the refrigerator cars had ridden down the tracks, watching for a "cooler."

As one passed, he urged his horse alongside. The animal kept pace with the moving car while its rider leaned over toward the door. Skillfully he broke the metal seal and yanked open one of the heavy insulated doors.

As the car came on toward the Hardys, one of their captors said, "Get ready to give 'em the heave-ho!"

The open car drew abreast. Frank and Joe were seized tightly, then heaved bodily up and into the yawning door of the moving refrigerator car. The heavy door slammed shut, and they could hear the bar fall into place on the outside.

Joe was first to come out of his daze. "Frank! We're locked in," he said hoarsely. "We'll freeze!"

His brother sat up and nodded. "Easy, Joe. We'll have to stay calm if we expect to get out of this alive."

Groggy, they stood up and tried to keep their balance in the pitch-black, chilly car. The only sound was the clackety-clack of the wheels. Frank took a small flashlight from his pocket and looked around. Their prison was filled with crates of West Coast lettuce.

Climbing up and over them, Frank presently came to the front wall of the car. It was damp and freezing cold against his hand.

"Joe! I just remembered something," he said hopefully.

"What?"

"Our scale-model trains. Refrigerator cars have ice compartments at each end, remember? Bunkers."

"That's right. The bunkers open into this section

near the roof, so the cold air can circulate. What about it?"

"That's our way out! Each bunker has a hatch in the roof, where ice is put in."

Staring upward by the dim light of the pocket flash, they could see that the open parts of the bunkers were covered by wire.

"If we can only cut through that!" Frank said.

"Here's my knife," Joe offered.

Climbing up on the stacked lettuce crates, Frank began hacking away at the wire screen. With only the light penknife, it took time, but finally he made a hole large enough to crawl through. Perched atop a steaming slippery cake of ice, he reached up for the hatch.

It was tightly locked.

"No luck," he called down in disappointment. Once back on the floor of the car, he added, "We have only one more chance—the other hatch."

"Let me try it this time," Joe suggested.

"Okay. Maybe you'll be luckier than I was."

With teeth chattering, Joe sawed away at the wire mesh of the other bunker and worked his way in on top of the ice. Anxiously he glanced up at the hatch. A thin sliver of light showed along one edge.

"Frank!" he shouted exultantly. "This one isn't locked!"

Quickly Joe leaned down over the edge of the bunker and helped Frank climb up into the ice chamber. Together they pushed at the hatch cover, but it didn't budge.

"Joe! All your might!" Frank urged. "This is our only chance!"

"My hands are so numb I can't even feel the hatch."

"We've got to make it!"

Bracing their shoulders and arms beneath the hatch, they gave one more mighty heave. This time they forced the cover upward and held it against the rushing wind, as they scrambled out.

A blast of wind nearly threw them off balance. But it was warm air and felt wonderful against their frigid skins.

"Duck down!" Frank yelled. "Less wind resistance. We'd better go up forward, toward the engine, to get some help."

As the Hardys inched forward, dusk began to come on. The train had topped a long grade, and was speeding now to make up for time lost on the hill. The boys swayed as the freight rounded a long curve.

Frank glanced back to see if he could spot any familiar landmarks. Consequently he did not see that up ahead loomed the black entrance to a tunnel. Joe saw it just in time.

"Frank! Get down!"

Falling flat, both boys hugged the roof of the refrigerator car as the train rolled into a long, vault-like tunnel cut through a mountain.

Several minutes later they emerged, choking and coughing from the exhaust fumes the Diesels had spewed into the tunnel. Despite the gravity of the situation, they couldn't help laughing. They were black with soot from head to toe.

"We sure look like a couple of free-hitching hobos!" Frank remarked.

Joe tried brushing the oily soot from his torn, frayed clothing, but it was no use. It simply smudged into the material and spread even more. He stopped suddenly and looked ahead.

"We're slowing down. Let's run forward and get some help from the crew."

Frank followed, wondering if their luck had changed at last.

CHAPTER XVII

Strong Man

AMID the rattle and banging of couplings, the long freight train jarred to a stop.

The boys, caught halfway between caboose and engine in their advance over the roofs of the careening cars, were thrown off balance and had to drop to their hands and knees to absorb the shock. But they arose at once.

"Now we can run up front," Joe cried out. "But hurry! This might be only a short stop."

Jumping from roof to roof, the boys shouted to attract the attention of any of the train crew who might be near. But no answering call came, and by the time they had covered a dozen cars the heavy freight gave a lurch and started up again, accelerating at an alarming rate. In a few minutes it was rolling even faster than before.

Joe, crouching and trying to flatten himself before the rush of air, cried, "Frank! The wind—it's terrific. I can—hardly—hold on!"

Frank himself was no better off. In a spread-eagled position behind Joe, he tried to brace himself on the swaying car top.

"Try—to—get—to—front. Grab—edge—of car!" Frank shouted.

Suddenly the gale carried a weird, piercing cry to their ears.

"That voice," Joe shouted. "Where is it coming from?"

They looked about, but there was no sign of anyone on the cars in front or behind them. Again the wind-whipped shout was heard.

"It's underneath us!" Frank yelled.

He slithered over near the edge of the roof and peered down. A rugged-looking, heavily-bearded face was gazing up from the car door. Its owner, a huge, broadly built man, held the boxcar door open with one hand and leaned out over the rushing roadbed to get a better view upward.

"Hey, you guys!" he shouted. "Wanta get kilt? Come down here. Feet first!"

Joe edged alongside Frank. "Friend or foe, we'll have to take the chance. We can't last much longer up here on the roof."

As Frank nodded, he twisted around so that his feet slid over the edge of the car. The screaming wind grabbed his body and swung it sideways as he carefully slid down. All at once he felt strong hands grab his legs in a tight grip. When his hands alon·

held him to the edge of the roof, Frank hesitated.

"Let go!" came the reassuring shout from below. "I've got you all right!"

With a sharp intake of breath, the boy released his hold. At that moment the car gave a sharp lurch, and for a moment Frank thought he would be hurled onto the roadbed.

But the man's grasp was more powerful than the boy had expected. He wrapped one leg around an upright stud and calmly lifted his human cargo safely into the car's interior.

"Thanks!" Frank murmured gratefully.

The man looked at him curiously, then leaned out and waved for Joe to follow. In a moment the younger Hardy was safe alongside his brother. Then, standing in the big car, dimly lighted by the butt of a candle set in an old tomato can, they faced the stranger.

He was as big as any man the boys had ever seen, well over six feet, and with broad shoulders and a deep chest.

"You two 'bos were ridin' the wrong part of the car," he boomed. "You ain't been around much or you'd know better. Ridin' the top o' a western freight just ain't done. They hit over fifty mile an hour."

"It felt like a hundred," Frank said. "I thought you'd never be able to hold onto us!"

"Nuthin' to it, nuthin' to it. Been liftin' weights

all my life. Used to be the strong man in Mercer Brothers Circus, until it folded up last year."

The man rolled his biceps like writhing snakes.

"I'm Kiko the Human Derrick," he continued. "Ever hear o' me?"

"No, we're Easterners. I don't think Mercer Brothers ever played out our way," Frank replied.

"Nah, we only hit the West. That's why you never caught my act. Too bad. I used to lift five hundred pounds like nuthin'!"

"That I wouldn't doubt," said Joe.

"Where you 'bos headed?" asked Kiko, changing the subject abruptly.

"Why, that's a question," Joe replied evasively. "We seem to be along for the ride. Where does this freight go?"

"Red Butte."

"How far is that?"

"A long way," the giant replied laconically, and lapsed into silence.

As the boys sat on the rough timber floor, listening to the clicking of wheels on rails, they wondered if they could possibly return to Spur Gulch in time to meet their father.

Joe, growing more and more fidgety, looked at his wrist watch. Despite the knocking about it had taken, it was still running, and by its luminous dial, he could see it was after ten o'clock.

"Not much time left to this day!" he remarked to

Frank. "And no way to keep our date with—" Joe caught himself just in time to bite off the word "Dad."

Aroused from his reverie by the boy's voice, Kiko noticed their restlessness.

"Say, what are you guys up to?" he asked. "I thought you weren't going anywhere in particular."

Frank was resolved not to let him in on any more of the situation than necessary. No telling which way his sympathies might lie in an emergency. It would be best to let Kiko think they were hobos.

"We just heard that a friend of ours was goin' to be at Spur Gulch," he said. "Know where that is?"

"Sure, just a coupla miles from here. We'll be goin' through there soon."

"Then let's get off," Joe said excitedly.

"That's what you think," Kiko muttered.

The brothers tensed. Having helped them once, did this giant now mean to block their way?

"What do you mean?" Frank asked uneasily.

"This train gallops through Spur Gulch like a wild bull on the loose. You won't be gettin' off there!"

"Where's the next upgrade?" Joe asked, knowing the train would slow down at that point.

"About a mile past the gulch. Yeah, maybe you could get off there."

As Kiko had foretold, they soon felt the train's pace slackening until it was pulling along at a very low speed.

"This is it," Frank said.

Kiko opened the heavy sliding door. The rough countryside of rocks and trees was plainly visible in the bright moonlight.

"Give me your hands, kids, and I'll let you down easy," Kiko offered.

"Thanks for your help," Frank said appreciatively. "Maybe we'll meet again sometime."

"Glad to do it. Us hobos got to help each other out—it's a tough enough life as it is."

Bracing himself against the door jamb, Kiko seized Joe's arms and held him out from the car's sides as easily as if he were a midget.

"Here comes a smooth spot!"

"Out on the sand!" yelled the big man, and eased Joe down on the smooth surface. A hundred yards down the track Frank followed. They could see Kiko in the doorway, waving and grinning broadly, and the Hardys yelled another thank-you.

"We sure were lucky to run into him," Joe remarked as they watched the freight disappear from view.

"Yes, a strong man in a circus, can you beat that?" Frank returned. "You meet strange people riding the rails."

Joe laughed. "I'll take a nice, comfortable Pullman chair, with a solid double window and air conditioning."

"Not now," Frank said seriously. "We have a good hike ahead of us back to Spur Gulch. It's nearly time for our date with Dad. I wonder if he's anywhere around?"

Taking a moment to survey the scene, the boys saw that they had dropped off the train about half-way up the grade. At its peak the freight had pulled around a curve, and then had vanished on a down-grade.

"Well, let's get moving," Joe suggested, and struck out in a westerly direction.

They had hardly hit their stride along the ties when Frank pulled up short.

"Look over there, Joe. In that patch of woods."

The orange-and-red light of a small campfire flickered through a thick grove of trees.

"Should we take time to see who's there?" Joe questioned. "After all, we're late now. Dad wants us at Spur Gulch. That campfire may belong to a gang of hobos—like Kiko."

"On the other hand," Frank reasoned, "Dad might be there himself."

Frank's argument convinced his brother, and the two boys left the right-of-way and moved cautiously toward the fire. It was no easy matter to force their way through the brush without signaling their advance. There had been no rain for a long time, and the footing was dry and covered with small branches and leaves.

Carefully placing each foot to avoid making any noise, the Hardys advanced among the trees. At the far edge of the grove in which the fire was located they paused in the underbrush and peered ahead.

A dozen men were huddled around the fire. One or two seemed to be eating. The others appeared to have finished their meal and were warming themselves near the blaze.

In the low buzz of conversation someone occasionally would make a wisecrack to provoke a chorus of rough laughter. Presently a deep voice which was raised above the rest gave the Hardys a chance to learn the subject of the men's conversation.

"Well, the boss and his new friend'll be here soon," the man rumbled. "Then the fireworks'll start!"

"Did you hear that, Frank?" Joe whispered. "This may be some sort of organized gang."

"*Sh-h-h* . . ."

"We can't wait for them much longer," another voice announced impatiently. "Number 68's due here in a little while."

"What's Number 68?" Joe muttered in his brother's ear. "One of the gang?"

"I'll bet it's the number of a train," Frank reasoned.

"You mean . . ."

"I mean I think these men may be train robbers. They're waiting to wreck Number 68 on the tracks right over there!"

"Then maybe we're not too late," Joe said hopefully. "Dad's probably around here somewhere. Let's get closer to these guys. Maybe we can hear exactly what they're up to."

The boys had crawled forward several feet when Frank gripped his brother's arm, pulling him to a stop. With his other hand cupped around Joe's ear, he whispered:

"It just occurred to me—that fellow mentioned the boss and his new friend. Do you think he could have meant Flint and Turk?"

CHAPTER XVIII

Thieves' Campfire

EDGING forward on their knees and elbows, the boys tried to get a better look at the faces of the men in the flickering firelight. One of them, his back to the Hardys, addressed the others.

"This reminds me of the job we pulled in Sacramento," he said. "Remember that one, Hank?"

"Yeah. Only that time it was a lead-pipe cinch. We didn't have no wise kids gettin' in the way of grown men."

The others laughed at his sarcastic tone.

"Can ya imagine a coupla high school kids holdin' up a deal like this?" the first speaker went on. "Well, we don't have to worry about them any longer. Flint said he'd take care of 'em before he got here."

Flint! The boys' deduction had been correct!

"At least," Frank told himself elatedly, "we're on the right track now."

The man called Hank spoke again.

"Me an' Pete was in the Sacramento job together. Knocked off a carload of automobile tires that time. We got a nice hunk o' cash for 'em, too."

Another man broke into the conversation with a raucous chuckle.

"I remember readin' about that one. I was back in New York, workin' for the state."

"You? When in blazes did you ever work for the state?" charged another voice with a loud cackle.

"Sure I was! Makin' license plates in the pen!"

At that there was a general guffawing. Then the big man called Pete stood up, stretching noisily.

"Me, I'm gettin' tired of waitin' around here. The sooner we get at this job, the better. I want to put the grab on those pipes and drills and then blow outta here."

"Sure," another agreed. "The quicker we get hold of that stuff, the quicker we can set up the diggin'."

"That goes for me," Hank agreed. "Flint said Number 68's got three cars loaded with the last word in oil rigs. We'll be rollin' in dough in a few weeks, and by that time it'll all be on the level."

Joe prodded Frank and the older boy knew what he was thinking. The stolen rig was to be set up in Wildcat Swamp after the land had been taken from Mrs. Sanderson!

"There's one thing I can't figure out," Frank

told his brother. "That government order for everyone to move out. Do you suppose these men don't know about it?"

"Could be. On the other hand, maybe that whole story was a fake to get rid of us."

"You mean that paper was a phony? But those rangers—"

"Phonies too!"

"In stolen uniforms."

Frank was about to say more when a sudden crackling in the woods startled him. Perhaps more of the gang was arriving, and the boys were on a direct line between them and the campfire!

Joe looked to Frank for instructions in this new dilemma.

"Too late to run!" Frank whispered. "Lie flat. Don't move!"

Face down in the undergrowth, they hugged the dry ground. The sound of heavy footsteps grew nearer. The newcomers passed the boys and approached the campfire. Conversation died abruptly. Frank and Joe looked up again momentarily, to see one of the men jump up, draw his pistol, and hurry away.

"Who's there?" he called, advancing to only a few feet from where the boys lay hidden.

Frank and Joe hardly dared to breathe until the challenger's attention was diverted by the two new arrivals who stepped into the firelight.

"What's the matter with you, Sam? Jumpy to-night?" one of them asked, in a low, controlled voice. Better dressed than any of the others, he presented an almost distinguished appearance.

The man with him was big and broad-shouldered. Even from where the Hardys lay squinting through the brush, they could see him frowning darkly at the others who now clustered around.

Instantly Frank and Joe recognized both of the newcomers. They were the men who had escaped from the Green Sand jail!

The boys listened tensely.

"Okay, Flint," replied Sam, ramming his pistol back into its holster. "It's this waiting that gets my nerves." Then, turning to the others, he added, "Meet your boss, men."

Flint was received enthusiastically. All the gang were eager to get their new job under way and the arrival of the boss meant that time for action was at hand.

Leading his companion into the center of the group, Flint said, "Men, I want all of you to meet an old pal of mine—Jesse Turk. He's going to be in on this caper with us."

"Okay by me," Hank said approvingly. "There's gonna be enough dough for everybody."

There was a murmur of assent and sardonic smiles spread over the faces of the group.

"Right!" Flint added. "This job is a lead-pipe

cinch. We had a little trouble getting rid of those Hardy kids. And then that fool fossil hunter—"

"What happened to him?" Hank questioned.

"He and the fat kid with him are tied up and hidden away in a cave—without food and water."

Involuntarily, the brothers winced at the thought of the gang's cruelty. Joe, in sudden anger, started to scramble to his knees, but Frank laid a firm hand on his arm.

"Take it easy, Joe. We can help Cap and Chet more by learning all we can here."

Though Frank had restrained him quickly, Joe's sudden movement had been heard by one of the men. A tall, hard-bitten member of the gang sprang to his feet.

"Boss, what was that over there? I swear I heard something move."

There was an ominous silence as the others listened too. The wind had died down and not a leaf stirred.

Suddenly the still night rang with a rasping laugh. It came from Turk, and his harsh amusement echoed through the woods. The rest stared at him.

"Flint, I thought you said you had men here!" he said bitingly. "These guys are nuthin' but a bunch of scared rabbits!"

There was an immediate and angry muttering among the group of thugs. Before it could develop into a fight, Gerald Flint stepped forward.

"All right, knock it off," he ordered briskly. "You guys have nothing to worry about. Those snooping Hardy kids have frozen to death in a cooler car, and their old man is next."

"You got him too?" Hank smirked.

"No, but we heard where he is. This job'll be a cinch now."

His authoritative demeanor having eased the tension, Flint drew Turk and Hank aside in a private conversation, while the others began talking of the robbery plans. Taking advantage of the general chatter, Frank nudged Joe.

"Back out of here," he proposed in a whisper.

Joe nodded and began inching his way backward through the brush. They had to get away—had to get to Spur Gulch, find their father, and warn him.

They had moved about half the distance to the edge of the grove when they heard Flint's voice giving more orders.

"Enough talk, men! Time to get moving. We've got a job to do before we can pull the holdup."

To the boys' horror the men picked up flashlights and began to tramp through the trees in their very direction.

"They'll spot us this time," Joe groaned. "How are we going to hide from all of them?"

Frank's quick mind hit upon an idea. "Hurry! Up a tree!"

Rapidly, before the beams of the flashlights could

reach them, he and Joe picked out two sturdy pine trees with low-hanging branches and shinned up into their thick foliage.

Seconds later the men pushed past beneath them and moved out of earshot.

"That was close," Joe muttered as they climbed down. "Now what?"

"It's better this way," Frank returned. "Now we can trail them."

Cautious at every step, the boys followed the gang, keeping well concealed. It was hard going without lights in the dark, cluttered woods, and their pace was slow compared to the men's.

Finally they saw the gang break out of the woods near the summit of the hill on which the boys had jumped off the freight cars. Beyond, the roadbed curved and descended in a long horseshoe.

"Let's go over there and watch," Frank said, pointing to a cluster of tall bushes down the track from where the men had emerged.

Halfway around the curve of the tracks, the thugs disappeared into the trees again. A moment later, when Joe was about to start after them, they reappeared, their flashlights bobbing as if they were carrying something.

"What have they got there?" Joe whispered.

"Looks to me like old railroad ties," Frank answered. "But what on earth—?"

His unfinished query was answered immediately

as the men heaved the great dried-out chunks of wood onto the tracks.

"When 68 hits that pile of ties it'll be derailed!" Frank exclaimed. "Then the gang will rob the freight cars."

"They've made a whopping big pile," Joe observed. "They really don't need all that to—"

"Joe! They're setting fire to it!"

A bright flame licked at the tinder-dry wood and in no time it had grown into a crackling blaze.

"They're not going to derail the freight, just stop it," Joe remarked. "Frank, we must warn the engineer!"

The boys started toward the oncoming freight. But at this moment Flint stepped into their path and shouted:

"It's burning fine, men. Here comes that rattler. To your jobs!"

Splitting into small groups, his henchmen disappeared into the night and Flint himself hurried off down the tracks toward the freight.

"Now's our chance," Joe said. "We may be caught, but we ought to make a try."

"We'll certainly be caught if we go that way," Frank objected. "Let's see if we can push those burning logs away so the train won't have to stop."

CHAPTER XIX

The Wreck

DASHING uphill as fast as their legs would carry them, the Hardys sped toward the pile of burning ties, which illuminated the night sky for a long distance. Reaching them, they found the center a roaring blaze, the heat intense.

Nevertheless, the two boys tugged frantically at the end of one of the heavy ties. At first it would not budge, and the brothers' faces were scorched before they managed to drag the heavy piece of wood away from the pyre. Its removal caused the others to collapse, sending sparks in every direction.

"It's no use!" Frank panted, beating off the sparks that singed his shirt. "We couldn't clear this away in time."

Their faces and arms smarting, and their eyes bloodshot, they were forced to move back.

"We'll have to try the other plan," Joe urged. "Come on!"

Frank was dubious of its success, but he followed

Joe. They hurried forward, jumping from tie to tie.

"I hope none of that gang's watching," Frank said. "If they see us, it's curtains."

Aided by the downgrade, the boys put a quarter mile between themselves and the fire before they saw the bright beam of the freight train's headlight. As the long train bore down on them with a roar, the Hardys took a determined stance in the middle of the track, waving their arms furiously. A second later the hoarse, warning honk of the Diesel's horn split the night in staccato blasts.

Still the boys held their position. The Diesel's air brakes suddenly were jammed on with a shriek, and the heavy freight ground to a stop. As the Hardys rushed toward the locomotive, the engineer leaned from the window, fury in every line of his face.

"Are you kids crazy?" he bellowed. "You could have been killed! What's the idea?"

"There's danger ahead!" Joe blurted, breathless.

"Train robbers!" Frank added.

In a space of a few seconds the Hardys impressed upon the engineer the necessity for speedy action. Turning, the man seized the induction telephone to the caboose, and frantically tried again and again to contact the men there.

"This is dead!" he cried. "There's no answer!"

Suddenly, from the other side of the big locomotive, came a rough command:

"Drop that phone and put up your hands!"

The engineer's eyes widened. Letting the instrument fall to the floor, he raised his hands, at the same time trying to nod to the boys to warn them.

There was nothing for Frank and Joe to do but to slip quietly into the brush along the tracks. From this cover, they peered up into the cab.

Two masked men were climbing into the compartment from the other side of the train, holding at gun point both the engineer and his fireman. Up the track, other members of the gang were using long hooks to remove the smoldering, red-hot ties that had formed the road block.

"Joe, if we cut through the woods, we can warn the crew in the caboose ourselves," Frank said excitedly.

"Let's do it!"

Stumbling blindly through the darkness on the inside of the horseshoe curve, the boys made their way toward the end of the long freight. They tripped over fallen logs, and whiplike branches cut their faces. In his haste, Joe caught his foot in a root and fell headlong. Frank helped him up, and they rushed on again.

"There are the lights of the caboose," Frank gasped. "Keep going!"

Guided now by the lights, they broke out of the woods and clambered up a short slope. With almost a sob of relief, Joe grabbed for the railing and clambered up the iron steps. Frank was right behind him. They had barely reached the platform on the tail end of the car when the train gave a sudden lurch.

"We're moving!" Joe yelled.

The next instant a voice, which was strangely familiar, shouted:

"Jump!"

The command carried so much authority that the boys obeyed instinctively. Leaping backward, they left the car and somersaulted down the cinder-packed embankment. Unhurt, they sprang quickly to their feet.

"The end of the train has broken loose!" Joe shouted.

The caboose and three big flatcars adjoining it had cut free and were rolling downgrade. The rest of the freight had started pulling ahead.

While the front section was slowly picking up speed, the four end cars were gathering momentum every second as they took the downhill curve.

"They'll derail!" Frank shouted. "The whole crew in the caboose will be killed!"

Hardly were the words off his lips when there was the sound of crunching steel, accompanied by flying sparks as the cars leaped the tracks.

With a tremendous roar, the cars toppled over the embankment. Their cargo slid off the toppling flatcars, scattering along the wooded right-of-way.

It was minutes before the din made by the falling pipes quieted down.

The Hardys started running toward the wrecked caboose, fearful of what they would find.

"We might have been on that!" Joe cried.

"Who yelled 'Jump'?" Frank asked.

"Say, I'd forgotten about that," Joe answered. "*Sh-h-h!*"

The whispered warning came from behind them. Wheeling about the boys saw a dim figure half hidden under a bush. A tall, strongly built man beckoned to them.

"Dad!" Frank and Joe exclaimed in one voice.

There was no time now to exchange stories. The three raced to the spot of the wreck, climbing around scattered pipes and splintered boxes.

"There's the caboose," Joe called. "The door has been ripped off!"

Quickly, all three pushed through the debris to the train crew's headquarters. Pulling themselves up its splintered sides, they peered down into the twisted, torn wreckage.

"There isn't anyone in it!" Mr. Hardy exclaimed. "Thank goodness you boys heard me and jumped in time."

"But where's the crew?" Joe asked. "The engineer was trying to get someone on that induction phone from the cab."

"They probably jumped out to see what was happening when you boys flagged the train," Mr. Hardy deduced. "They may have been coming up along the embankment when the last four cars started rolling."

"In that case, the crew should be around here somewhere," Frank said.

"Yes, but most of these freights today are sadly undermanned," Mr. Hardy stated. "I doubt very much if they would be a match for such a well-organized gang as this one. Now the question is, did those cars break loose, or did someone uncouple them?"

"They were wrecked on purpose," Frank answered, and told his father all that had happened since he and Joe had reached Wildcat Swamp; how they had overheard that Flint was boss of the gang; how Cap and Chet were prisoners in a cave and starving; and all, the boys believed, because the ex-convicts wanted to drill for oil illegally on Mrs. Sanderson's land.

"We'll rescue Chet and Cap as soon as we can," Mr. Hardy decided. "They'll have to hold out awhile. First we must do something about this gang here, and it's going to be tough without help."

"Are you alone, Dad?" Joe asked.

"Sam Radley is out here working with me, but all our tips pointed to Spur Gulch as the trouble spot. He was bringing a posse to meet me there. But now that you've told me about the oil drilling, I can see why Flint picked this place. These three cars contain the materials they need. There's a rough woods road near here over which they can drag the stuff."

"Dad, how'd it happen you're in this spot alone?" Frank asked.

"Jack Wayne flew me in. The only level spot on the mountain was about half a mile from here. I originally planned to walk to Spur Gulch along the tracks.

"On the way, I came almost face to face with some of this gang, and couldn't get past them. What I have been doing is taking pictures with our infrared camera of all of these thugs I can get close to. We'll have quite a record of—"

A shot rang out, then another. A moment later two uniformed trainmen came racing in their direction, followed by two of the robbers. Mr. Hardy, whipping out his own revolver, was about to go to the assistance of the trainmen when six more armed thugs came into view.

"We're outnumbered," the detective said in disgust. "Our only chance to capture that gang now is by a trick."

The Hardys hugged the trees to keep from being seen, but even from his hiding place, the detective kept clicking his camera.

"This is all good evidence," he whispered grimly. "When we get this mob into court, the jury won't take long to convict every one of them."

Frank and Joe had no doubt of their father's

ability to outwit the gang eventually, but at this moment the situation looked desperate. Besides, all three of them were in danger of being captured.

"Keep under cover," the detective warned as Joe stepped out. "This is no time to be discovered."

The words were hardly out of his mouth when their hiding place became flooded with light!

160   The Secret of Wildcat Swamp

CHAPTER XX

The Rough Ride

SIX bright beams of light swept the Hardys hiding place from the opposite side of the tracks. As they drew closer, the Hardys could make out two low-slung open trucks, each with a powerful spotlight, in addition to glaring headlights.

"Great crow!" Joe exclaimed. "Where did they come from?"

"Over the abandoned logging road," his father replied. "More of Flint's smart organization work. Those trucks can carry the pipes and oil well equipment out of here easily."

"Can't we do something?" Frank said desperately, as the trucks lurched across the rails and halted alongside the wrecked cars.

"I think so," his father said coolly. "I'm going to trick Flint and try to capture him."

The detective turned to his sons. "You boys take note of what's going on here. Wait until the next train passes through. That'll be at nine A.M. The robbers will have left long before that. Stop the train and ride to Red Butte. I'll meet you there at noon."

Reaching into his jacket, the detective pulled out a small bottle. "Concentrated food tablets," he said, handing them to Frank. "You may need them. Good-by."

Leaving his sons, Mr. Hardy crawled through the bushes until he was in heavy cover. Then he stood up cautiously. Returning to the tracks, he walked upgrade a considerable distance from the scene of the robbery.

When the detective was sure he could not be seen by the men loading the boxes and pipes onto the trucks, he crossed the tracks. Easing back to the scene slowly, he spotted two figures who stood on a rise, silhouetted against the night sky. Mr. Hardy moved within hearing distance.

"Worked like a charm, Turk," one of the men said. "I uncoupled the last four cars and clamped the air brake on the forward section, so the rest of the train could move ahead as soon as Pete got the burned ties off the tracks."

"Flint, you're a brain. We ought to have this load out of here within an hour."

With a grim smile on his lips, Mr. Hardy suddenly stepped into the open.

"Flint!" he shouted.

The two train robbers whirled about. The shutter of the detective's camera clicked twice. Turk beamed his flashlight as Mr. Hardy ducked.

Flint cursed, whipped a pistol from his shoulder holster, and fired a clip of bullets at the spot where the detective had stood a second before.

"It's Fenton Hardy!" Flint roared. "Turk, you supervise the men. Lend me your light. I'm going to get this dick if it's the last thing I ever do!"

As soon as the detective saw Flint coming after him, he drew back into the wooded area and headed for Jack Wayne's airplane. Although he could have escaped pursuit, Mr. Hardy deliberately let Flint catch an occasional glimpse of him, leading the gang leader farther away from his gang.

Flint's rage increased as Frank and Joe's father tormented him with a dangerous game of cops and robbers. Once, when Flint drew near, the detective threw a stone, which landed behind the ex-convict. The criminal whirled and fired blindly. When he did, the detective abandoned his concealed position and plunged noisily ahead, with Flint rampaging after him.

Half an hour later Mr. Hardy emerged from the woods into a clearing, in the center of which stood Jack Wayne's airplane. Running toward it, the detective shouted:

"Jack! Flint's right behind me. Cover me while I give him a whiff of the gas gun!"

As a face appeared in the pilot's window, the detective stopped short. Instead of Jack Wayne's familiar features, he saw in the moonlight a thin face with a large sharp nose and eyes like black marbles. An unknown enemy was facing him and Flint was only a few steps behind!

Meanwhile, the detective's sons had continued to watch the well-planned and executed theft of the oil well drilling equipment. The freight's conductor and brakeman were being kept covered.

In an hour the two trucks were loaded and the cargoes concealed with heavy tarpaulins. Two men climbed into each cab and the others faded into the woods along with their prisoners.

"So long!" one driver called. "See you at Wildcat Swamp after we deliver this stuff to Willie and Snide."

Frank and Joe exchanged startled glances. Now the jigsaw pieces were dropping into place. Willie the Penman! But who was Snide?

The Hardys' nerves tingled. "Frank, are we going to stand here and do nothing?" Joe cried.

"No, sir. Come on!" Frank muttered. "We'll ride back to Wildcat Swamp and free Cap and Chet."

"How about meeting Dad?"

"We'll get there—maybe just a bit late."

As the trucks pulled away, the boys ran across the track. Racing down the other side, they found the narrow overgrown road, then began following the second truck's taillights.

Fortunately, the loaded vehicles were forced to crawl along the twisting logging road. Jogging alongside, Joe was able to untie a corner of the tarpaulin and boost himself aboard the load of loose steel pipes. He pulled Frank up after him, and the boys retied the canvas over them. As the truck rolled and pitched through the night, Frank whispered:

"From the feel of the grades and turns, we're still on the logging road."

"It's rough going," Joe replied. "I wish they'd picked a smoother route."

With each big lurch and bump, the pipes clanged and slithered into new positions. The boys fought to keep their balance and avoid being pinched between portions of the cargo.

After what seemed hours, the truck groaned to a stop. Another vehicle approached at high speed and roared past, the sound of its whining tires fading in the distance.

"We must have reached the main highway," Frank deduced.

A moment later the truck edged onto a smooth pavement.

"Thank goodness for this," Joe whispered.

The driver shifted into high gear, and the vehicle rumbled along smoothly. Despite the boys' discomfort, the harrowing experiences of the day and night were making them drowsy. After what seemed to be hours, Joe awoke with a start. He reached out and found his brother's arm in the dark.

"Frank! Wake up! We've stopped!"

Joe found a tiny hole in the canvas and peeked through it.

"We're at a diner," he whispered. "The driver and his helper are going to the door. The other truck's parked ahead of us."

Frank drew his penknife and cut a small peephole. "They're probably stopping for a cup of coffee," he whispered. "When they get inside, let's go in the back way and phone the police."

Joe crawled to the rear of the truck and began untying the cover. He had a leg over the side when Frank grabbed his shoulder.

"Get back! They're coming out!"

Their two drivers, one of them fairly young, approached the truck, accompanied by a third man. Hearing them walk toward the back of the vehicle the boys eased forward and slid between the pipes and some boxes, just as the tarpaulin was lifted, letting in a slit of light.

"We got it, all right," said a voice the boys recognized as that of the driver. "The whole works."

"What's that up there in front?" the man from the diner asked.

The boys held their breaths.

"Boxes of drill bits and fittings."

As the three men stood talking, it became evident that the newcomer owned the diner. As the cover was tied down again, he said:

"I got a report from Flint already."

"So quick? What'd he say?"

"Buzzed me on his pocket radio. He'll be along soon. Said that when the trucks reached here to tell you that he and Fliegel captured Fenton Hardy and his pilot."

The words came like an electric shock to the boys. Flint had turned the tables and captured their father!

"Man, that was fast work!" the driver said with a hoarse laugh. "Flint just told us back at the railroad he had a plan for getting Hardy."

"Well, he did it. Must've done a real job on him, too. Flint said the dick needs a doctor, but he ain't getting one! You get started. I'll take a look at the other truck."

Frank and Joe were frantic with worry. Their father was injured and needed help, and here they were, powerless to aid him. However, they knew that becoming panicky would do no good. They must think of something!

As the truck started on the highway again, Joe said, "Frank, we'd better get off the first chance we have. We'll find a ranch house and call the police. We've got to find Dad!"

"You're right."

The brothers watched through the holes in the

canvas. But they passed no ranch houses and the truck sped through the night at high speed. The boys suddenly heard the younger driver say to his companion:

"You know, I don't trust that flat-nosed Snide. I think he'd double-cross the lot of us in a minute, if he had the chance."

Joe's elbow dug into Frank's side. Flat-nosed! One of the phony rangers had had a flat nose!

"But you gotta remember, Charlie," the other man in the front seat was saying, "Snide's a good oil man. He'll be useful to have around on a deal like this."

There was a snort from his companion.

"I don't care—I'd rather do without him. He's too ready to go to extremes. He woulda killed one of those kids without battin' an eye, and I just can't go that far."

"Bah! What're you doin', gettin' soft?"

"No, but we can put this whole thing across without murder, can't we?"

"Aw, can it! Anybody gets in our way deserves what he gets. And Nick Snide'll be the guy to give it to 'im."

There was a growl of disagreement from the younger man, but apparently he could not see much sense in continuing the argument. The men lapsed into silence.

"That young helper doesn't sound like such a bad

sort," Frank whispered to Joe as they crouched listening. "How'd he get mixed up with a gang like this?"

Joe had only time to shrug when they felt the truck slow down and turn off the smooth highway onto a bad road. The wheels alternately crunched over loose stone and slid through yielding sand.

It was perilous going. The Hardys were forced to move from behind the crates and crouch on top of the load. As the truck hit a bad bump, the younger man shouted:

"Hey, watch it! This ain't no super highway!"

"Calm down," said the driver irritably. "It's only ten miles to the swamp."

"Just the same," the other said, "there ain't no reason to set a record. We passed the other truck an hour ago."

The truck lurched over, its right wheels slipping sideways. "Watch that ditch!"

"Aw, shut up! You been a pain in the neck ever since we started this job."

"I don't like what's goin' on. If—"

The driver suddenly yanked the wheel. The big vehicle skidded. The load shifted sharply, sending an avalanche of pipe toward Frank and Joe!

CHAPTER XXI

A Friendly Outlaw

"Look out, Frank!" The warning shout slipped from Joe involuntarily.

Reaching high, the boys grabbed the cross braces, and pulled themselves up just as the heavy sections of pipe crashed across the floor of the truck.

The big vehicle skidded to the side of the road, shuddering as it hit the soft shoulder, and stalled.

"Now you've done it," they heard the helper berate the driver. "If we get stuck here, the boss'll—"

"Shut up!" the angry driver commanded. "Didn't you hear that yell? Somebody's in the back of this truck!"

"Aw, you're loco."

"Listen, bud, I heard somethin', and I'm checkin' up."

With a mad scramble Frank and Joe slid from under the tarpaulin and landed in the road. Quietly they ducked underneath the truck's chassis, just as the husky driver swaggered down from his seat in the cab.

Back along the side of the truck he walked, the boys watching his feet every bit of the way. Leaning over the tailboard, he fumbled with the canvas tarpaulin. Joe looked at the man's legs, so near his own hidden shoulder.

"Too good to miss!" he thought.

Reaching out his arms, he grabbed the back of the driver's legs and yanked them forward. There was a startled *umph* as the fellow went crashing to the road. His gun went one way and his flashlight another. Before he could yell to his pal, the two boys were upon him. Joe brought his fist swinging hard to the man's jaw, and he collapsed without a sound.

Desperately, the brothers dragged his inert form under the truck. They were not a second too soon.

"Well, did you find anything?" Charlie called as he climbed out on the other side of the cab.

Receiving no answer, he stalked to the rear of the vehicle to investigate. Frank set himself to duplicate his brother's action. His shoulder hit the man just below the knees, and before he knew what was happening to him, Joe had contributed the knockout blow.

"What are we going to do with them?" Joe put the situation up to Frank.

"I don't know yet, but we'll have to do something fast. Look!"

Down the road, still a good distance away, two bouncing pin points of light became visible. The other truck was catching up with them!

"Come on, we'll drag these fellows into the tall grass there." Frank indicated the high growth on the other side of the road, and quickly they tugged the two unconscious men out of sight.

"We'd better run," Joe advised.

Frank had another plan. "We don't want them to stop. Let's put on their caps and pull 'em down. They'll hide our faces a little, and maybe we can get by."

"All right. You get in the cab. I'll pretend I'm tying this canvas, and you wave them on from the window," Joe suggested.

By this time the beams of the other truck's headlights were almost upon them. Frank climbed as casually as he could into the cab and sat there with his left hand giving the passing signal. Joe fussed with the canvas on the side of the truck away from that on which the other vehicle would pass.

Those few seconds seemed an eternity to the boys as the second truck rolled up to them, but it never hesitated. There was shouted ridicule about "lazy coyotes," but the driver kept his foot pressed down on the accelerator.

The scheme had worked!

"We'd better get back to those two we hid, and tie 'em before they wake up," Frank said, leaping from the cab.

Using the rope with which the canvas had been tied, they first secured the driver's wrists and ankles. Just as he was coming to, they managed to gag him firmly.

"We'd better drag him back where there's no possible chance of his rolling into the road and having one of the gang find him," Joe proposed. The driver was dragged off and wedged into a cluster of trees that made movement of any sort almost impossible.

"How about Charlie?" Joe asked. "I'll get more rope."

"Wait!" Frank said. "I've been thinking about Charlie. He sounded as if he's pretty tired of the gang. Do you suppose we could persuade him—?"

The young man was just beginning to show signs of regaining consciousness when the boys returned to him. Frank removed Charlie's pistol a split second before he sat up and shook his head.

"What happened?" he groaned.

When his head had cleared, the boys revealed their identity.

"But I thought you were—"

"Frozen to death in that refrigerator car?" Joe finished grimly. "No, your boss just wasn't smart enough."

"I'm glad of that!" he growled. "I told those hombres they were goin' too far."

"Listen, Charlie," Frank began earnestly, "you don't seem to be a bad sort. Why don't you quit this gang right now?"

"You could go straight, and give us a hand in the bargain," Joe urged.

"How?" Charlie asked suspiciously.

"If you help us turn the tables on those thieves, we'll do everything we can to clear you with the police."

"But if you stick with them," Frank said, "the way things are going, they're bound to wind up in prison for life."

Charlie was silent, looking first at the Hardys and then off into the distance, as he thought the proposition over.

"You're right," he said at last. "Now's my chance. Maybe you won't believe me, but I just hooked up with Flint. Lure of easy money. I ain't done anything yet to get me a sentence." He paused a few seconds. "I got two kid brothers your age. If I get caught— Well, I guess I'll have to trust you about helping me out, later on. But first, what can I do for you?"

Elated over this unexpected source of assistance, the boys helped Charlie to his feet and discussed the situation.

"Somebody's got to find out about our dad,"

Frank said. "Flint told that fellow back at the diner that Dad needed a doctor. He must be hurt! Where's Flint?"

"He's coming to the diner," Charlie answered.

"How about your going back there and finding out about Dad?" Frank asked. "Then you can notify the police."

"Sure. I'll conk the owner and then wait for Flint to come along."

"How about this driver tied up? Can you take care of him?" Frank asked.

"I'll send somebody out to bring him in," Charlie promised. "Don't worry. You can count on me. I don't want to end up in the chair!"

It was decided that the boys would drive on to the swamp, while Charlie would walk to the main highway and hitch a ride back to the diner. As proof of the boys' confidence in him, Frank gave the man his gun.

As he set off down the rough trail, the boys climbed into the cab of the truck. Frank drove at a more careful speed than the previous driver had.

"How close do you think we ought to get to that gang?" Joe asked.

"Not too close. We'll sneak up on foot and find out where they're taking this equipment."

"Then we'll head for the cave to help Cap and Chet," Joe added as they bumped and jounced along.

After that, the boys drove in silence until they saw lights ahead. Frank slowed the truck to a crawl.

"They're unloading the stuff," he said. "I would guess they are at the top of the slope above Wildcat Swamp, just opposite where we are digging."

Several men were busy carrying lengths of pipe and heavy boxes which they were piling behind some bushes. Fortunately no one turned around when Frank braked to a complete stop.

"Now's our chance to get away!" Joe urged. They quickly climbed out and hurried into the shadows.

By this time streaks of gray were showing in the eastern sky. With the breaking dawn to help them, the brothers picked their way toward the swamp. Knowing that the thieves would be camping somewhere near it, they gave the swamp a wide berth as they made their way toward the sloping bank where they had been digging.

They were skirting the swamp when Joe suddenly stopped to listen intently. In the distance there was a low hum and rumble.

"The trucks, Frank! They must have finished unloading. They're leaving."

"I hope Charlie gets to the diner before they do. That gang's surely discovered by this time that he and the driver of the second truck are missing. They're probably searching for them right now."

Hopeful, they pushed on around the swamp,

finally completing a tortuous half circle that brought them to the bottom of the sandy slope in which the camel fossil was buried.

"Say," said Joe, as he reached the entrance to the cave, "what have they done to this place? It's choked with sand and rocks!"

"The gang must have done it to hide the entrance from strangers," Frank replied. "I wonder if the other entrance—."

Hurriedly they rushed around to the other end of the slope. The entrance there had been treated in exactly the same way.

"No choice here—they're both bad," Joe announced. "The other entrance will be easier to negotiate."

They returned to it, scrambling over the pile of sand and gravel to reach the cave opening. But before entering, Frank threw the strong beam of his flashlight as far into the cave as it would carry.

"Cap! Chet!" Joe called.

There was no answer.

"Come on, Frank!"

After a breath-taking slide, they landed in the mouth of the deep cavern, and flashed their lights around the chamber. There was no sign of Cap and Chet.

Dismayed and filled with apprehension, Frank began a search of the inner room. "There may be a deeper section to this cave than we thought."

Seconds later Joe heard his cry of joy. "They're here!"

Lying in a crevice beneath the far wall, bound and gagged, were their friends. In no time, the brothers had Cap and Chet out in the central portion of the cave.

"I'll get the gags off," Joe said excitedly. "You untie their hands."

With his pocketknife he sliced the tight, coarse kerchiefs with which the captives had been gagged. Even when the gags were removed, Cap and Chet could barely whisper. They were very weak, saying they had had no food since being captured.

After all their bonds were removed, the two found that because of their long inactivity, they could not stand up. Frank and Joe massaged their numbed arms and legs to restore circulation, and in a little while the released prisoners were able to hobble painfully, a couple of steps at a time.

"Eat some of these food tablets," Frank said. "They'll help until we can get some more solid food."

A few minutes later Cap and Chet were able to give a halting, whispered account of their capture by the phony rangers.

The brothers burned with anger when they were told that the scoundrels had come back a second time to gag their captives and bind them even more securely.

"It was then," Cap continued with parched lips, "that they tried to seal off the entrances to the cave. They said nobody, not even the Hardys, would ever see us alive again."

"I'd like to get my hand on that Willie just once more," Chet muttered.

"Easy does it," Joe advised. "Come on now. We have to get out of here."

It took a long time and lots of perseverance for the brothers to get their friends out of the sand-choked passageway, but eventually, all four stood on the ledge at the top of the slope. Cap and Chet, accustomed for so long to the darkness of the cave, were almost blinded by the early morning light.

"Listen, Frank," said Joe, "they're in no condition to walk. I'll get their horses, while you stay here with them."

Cap laid a hand on Frank's arm.

"No use!" he said in a tired, discouraged voice. "The men took our horses. We're stranded!"

CHAPTER XXII

Double-crossed

FRANK shot a startled glance at Joe. The Hardys knew the seriousness of the situation and Cap sensed it too.

"You boys go ahead," he told them. "Chet and I will take it easy and get there when we can."

"But the horses," Chet spoke up. "You can't go far in this country without horses."

"I have it," Joe cried. "Our pack mule! He was well hidden. If the thieves didn't take him, Frank and I will ride it to Red Butte and send horses back to you."

"Our nearest point to contact the law," Cap suggested, "is Sheriff Paul."

"We never did find out what happened at his home," Frank reminded his brother. "Suppose we see if he has returned. On their way back to Red Butte, Cap and Chet can stop at the Sanderson ranch to see if everything is all right there."

Leaving Cap and Chet hobbling slowly along, the

Hardys made for the camp site to look for the pack animal. It was grazing peacefully in a little natural corral. The boys threw a blanket across the mule's back and mounted.

For a moment the amazed beast stood still. Then, at a signal from Frank's heel, it plodded up the slope. Reaching the trail, the animal ignored a signal to turn right and doggedly trudged toward Wildcat Swamp. No amount of coaxing could change its mind.

"Now what are we going to do?" Joe asked impatiently.

"It's just possible," Frank reflected, "that our mule has been used by someone else and is taking the route he's become accustomed to. The beast may lead us to a new clue."

The boys rode along without attempting to guide the animal. It headed straight for the defile, went through it, and stopped just above the spot where Cap and the boys had been digging.

"Well, what do you make of this?" Joe asked, perplexed.

Frank jumped off and started down the slope, waving to Joe to follow.

"Somebody else has been digging here—they even put up a sign!" he cried.

Joe scrambled closer to the sign.

"DANGER," he read aloud. "EXPLOSIVES BURIED. KEEP OUT."

"I wonder if that's a trick to scare us away from here," Frank pondered.

"We'd better not stop to find out," Joe replied. "But I think we should warn Chet and Cap in case it's true."

This time the mule willingly carried the boys in the opposite direction. Reaching camp, he turned in.

"Somebody sure has been using this mule recently," Frank said. "I wonder if it was to carry dynamite."

"Sure looks like it if the sign means anything," Joe answered.

At that moment Cap and Chet wearily arrived at the camp.

"What's up now? I see you found the mule, but why did you come back?" Chet asked.

Quickly the Hardys explained and urged their friends to stay away from the pit.

When Cap agreed, Frank and Joe started off again. Reaching the trail, their mule once more turned left.

"Oh, no, not again," Joe cried, trying his best to guide the animal to the right.

"Now what?" Frank pondered. "It's a long walk to Sheriff Paul's."

Joe broke a leafy twig from a sapling and remounted. "Frank, you walk ahead the way we want to go. I'll see what I can do from here."

His brother took the lead rope and started. The mule walked four steps, then stopped. Joe tickled its ear with the twig. As the mule's attention was distracted, Frank coaxed it a few feet farther.

This maneuver continued until the beast seemed to lose interest in going back. There was no more trouble and Frank climbed up behind his brother.

Meanwhile, Cap and Chet were at a loss about how to shake the dust of the camp from their tired feet. Without horses they certainly would not be able to go far.

Sitting before their tent, Cap's far-roving eye spotted a movement on the hillside. A herd of wild horses was moving across the hill, stretched out in a long, broken line of twos and threes. Peculiarly, almost all of them stopped abruptly at one point on the slope. Then each small group moved on, to be replaced by another.

"What are they looking at?" Chet murmured, ambling to the teacher's side.

"I'm not sure, but I'm beginning to work up a hunch!" Cap said. "Come on down here with me."

As they jolted down the incline, Cap let out a cry. "I was right! Our horses!"

There were the two mounts that Chet and Cap had hired, tethered in a grove of pine trees and grazing calmly.

"So this is where those phony rangers hid them," Chet exclaimed.

"Now we can do a little traveling of our own!" Cap cheered. "Let's get started for the Sanderson ranch."

Stiffly they swung into the saddles, and a minute later were loping along the trail in the direction of the ranch.

While all this was happening, Frank and Joe were still swaying from side to side on the back of the mule. Heading in another direction, they set no such pace as Cap and Chet. Without a horse to follow, the mule ambled along at a pace of his own choosing.

After three hours of stumbling over sand-covered rocks and sliding along bare shale, the mule brought the boys in sight of the sheriff's ranch.

"I hope somebody's here," Joe said, "to give me a tall glass of water."

Dismounting, the boys discreetly tied the mule behind the barn and went to the door of the ranch house.

"Hello!" they called. No answer.

"Looks exactly as it was before," Frank said, pushing the door open.

Seeing their note still lying on the table, the boys went through to the kitchen. The unwashed dishes still rested in the sink and the basket of clothes remained untouched.

"It's a sure thing that Mrs. Paul hasn't been back here," Joe said. "Shall we try it to Red Butte once more?"

"Yes, but through open country. I don't want to be stopped again."

As the two boys crossed the living room, Joe noticed something strange. "Say, the radiotelephone's gone," he said.

"That means somebody *has* been here since we left," Frank reasoned.

Before the Hardys could ponder the riddle further, a distant clatter of hoofs caused them to glance out the window. Three riders in green uniforms were galloping up to the house.

"The fake rangers!" Frank warned. "We'd better get out of here."

The brothers hurried through the kitchen, closing the back door quietly behind them, then crossed the yard rapidly and hid inside the stone-and-rail corral attached to the barn.

No sooner had they concealed themselves than the men, who were masked, galloped up and dismounted. After glancing about they apparently decided that they were alone and removed their masks.

Through a crack in the corral fence, the boys could see that one of the men was short, scrawny, beady-eyed Willie the Penman! The flat-nosed, fierce-looking man with the craggy brows must be Nick Snide, they surmised.

Willie gave a laugh of satisfaction. "This is a snap with the sheriff out of the way, Snide," he said. "He sure bit on that 'missing rangers' gag."

"Willie," Snide said, "I have to hand it to you The sheriff walked right into that one. Nobody'd ever think to look for him in the tower."

Nudging his brother, Joe whispered, "Wonder where this tower is they're talking about?"

Willie's whining voice continued. "We can't stick around here long. I'll get those seals I'll need to make the papers look legal. Somebody might—in fact, somebody *is* coming. It's that Sanderson kid. Quick! Take off those uniforms. Pretend you're waiting for the sheriff. I'll hide in the barn."

Frank and Joe watched Willie's companions strip off the rangers' uniforms, revealing cowboy outfits underneath. Willie carried the discarded clothes through the open barn door.

Harry rode up to the men, who greeted him in a friendly manner.

"I'm looking for the sheriff," the boy said. "I need his help."

"We're waiting for Paul ourselves," Snide answered. "What's your trouble?"

Frank and Joe clenched their fists, hoping the boy would say no more. But Harry continued earnestly:

"Well, a couple of days ago, a man and three boys promised me they'd help Mom find a way to keep her land. Then they went into Devil's Swamp and disappeared. I want Sheriff Paul to help me find them."

"No use," Snide said. "Two of 'em named Frank and Joe told me they were going back to their home in a place called Bayport. You might as well go home yourself. Just wasting your time here."

Harry looked surprised when he heard the Hardys mentioned, but still seemed undecided. "I've got to see the sheriff," he insisted.

"I'll give him your message, kid."

"Well, okay." The boy wheeled his horse and rode slowly past the corral on his way out.

"Now's my chance," Joe whispered to Frank.

Crouching low and running as quietly as possible, he came to the far corner just as Harry did and peered through the bars.

"Pretend you don't see me, Harry," he said in a loud whisper. The boy stiffened. "I'm Joe Hardy. Get off your horse and act as if you're tightening the cinch."

Without looking toward Joe's hiding place, the boy dismounted and began adjusting his saddle.

"You've got to get to Red Butte for help," Joe continued. "These men are in with the gang that's after your land! They're holding Sheriff Paul in a tower. Hurry!"

Harry played his part well. He nodded slightly, mounted his horse, and trotted away. Leaving the ranch, he spurred the animal into a gallop. Harry realized that no time was to be lost. The boy rode at breakneck speed for a mile, then slowed down slightly to rest his horse.

About to resume his fast pace, Harry saw two riders approaching. They guided their horses on either side of him and one man grabbed his reins.

"Whoa there, kid," the larger of the two husky riders said. "Where are you going in such a rush?"

"To town," Harry blurted out. "There's a gang of crooks trying to steal Mom's land and they're holding Sheriff Paul a prisoner!"

"How'd you find all this out?" the other man asked.

"Joe Hardy told me. He and his brother Frank are hiding at the ranch right now. You've got to help us!"

"Oh, we'll give you a hand, all right." He turned to his big companion. "Give him both hands!"

The man seized Harry's wrists and tied them behind his back. He lashed the boy around the waist to the high Western pommel of his saddle and hobbled his horse with a length of rope. The animal would be able to move only a few inches with each step.

Harry's eyes were wide with fright. "What's the idea? You must be—"

"That's right, kid," the big man said. "You talk too much to the wrong people."

Leaving Harry helpless, the men then whipped their horses and galloped on toward the Paul ranch.

Back in the corral, Frank and Joe were still crouching behind the fence. Willie the Penman had gone into the ranch house, but the others remained outside.

There was the clatter of hoofbeats, and on both sides of the corral wall behind which the Hardys were hiding there was a dash for cover. The boys simply crouched lower; the fake rangers ran behind the house.

"Two men!" Joe whispered, peering between the bars at a pair of riders cantering toward the house. "They can't be reinforcements sent by Harry. It's too soon for that."

When Willie and his henchmen recognized the newcomers, they stepped out to meet them. The men spoke in low tones that did not carry to the corral fence.

"This doesn't look good!" Joe warned. "Look! They're fanning out all over the place as if to cut off our escape."

"Snide is coming this way!" Frank exclaimed, crouching lower.

Stalking cautiously around the corner of the fence where Joe had talked to Harry, Snide turned along its near side. As he reached the end, the brothers quietly retreated toward the barn. A few yards more and they could make a run for it.

Suddenly there was a shout from behind them. "There they are!"

Whirling, the boys found two big cowboys between them and the barn.

Snide ran toward them from the other side.

Frank and Joe were trapped!

CHAPTER XXIII

An Untimely Explosion

SNIDE, seeing the Hardys, twisted his mouth to one side and called:

"Come on, Willie!"

There was a heavy stomping of cowboy boots as the wiry little figure of Willie the Penman suddenly rounded the corner, followed by a hulking cowboy.

"They're right here," Snide yelled. "Been here all the time. The meddlin' Hardys!" Then, with his eyes narrowed, he shouted, "Get 'em!" and charged at Frank and Joe.

The boys delivered a couple of stiff one-two punches before they went down in a melee of arms and legs. But they were fighting against hopeless odds. Backed up against the corral fence, they were unable to move, and the battle was over almost before it began.

Wiping the sweat from his face, Willie stood before the brothers, held firmly in viselike grips by his companions.

"So you got out of the cooler, eh?" he whined in his high-pitched voice. "Well, wise guys, you won't outsmart us again!"

Turning to the other men, he issued one crisp order:

"Tie 'em up—tight!"

Going into the barn, two of them found lengths of bailing wire. Twisting it roughly around the boys' wrists and ankles, they made certain that Frank and Joe could not move.

Willie was now ready to consider the brothers as disposed of as they lay in the dirt and dust of the ranch corral. He announced that he had more important matters on his mind. Facing Snide again, he said:

"I'm ready to take off. Just be sure these kids don't pull any fast ones on you. Keep 'em tied and under guard. I don't want to come back and find 'em gone again."

"Don't worry," his companion replied. "They're going to stay put."

"Okay. I'm late now. Mrs. Sanderson will be heartbroken if I don't keep our little date." The forger snickered sarcastically.

There were hoots from the others of the gang. "Yeah, she'll sure be glad to see you," one of them said sardonically. "All it will cost her is her ranch and a lot of dough."

Snide raised a hand of caution, and the speaker subsided.

"Sure you got all the papers for her to sign, Willie?" Snide asked. "Now that we're gettin' this close, we don't want no slip-up with the law."

"Sure—sure. I'm no amateur," Willie said, annoyance in his voice. "She'll sign everything legal and proper. If she don't, I'll coax her a little. I'll tell her about Harry!"

The boys looked at each other in mystified silence. What had Willie meant by that? Was Harry Sanderson in trouble? If he were, that would mean he had not delivered their message for help.

But no explanation was forthcoming from the gang. Snide and Willie, standing off from the others, exchanged a few last-minute instructions. Then Willie called for one of the horses, and rode off in the direction of the Sanderson ranch.

The rest watched until he was out of sight, whereupon Snide turned his attention to the Hardy brothers.

"That takes care of Willie's department," he said to no one in particular. "Now we'll see about mine."

He prodded Joe with a foot. "How'd you jerks get here, anyway?" he rasped.

Receiving no answer, he continued, "Oh, more heroic guys, eh, like your friends in the cave? Well, we'll—" He was interrupted by a sudden shout. "Hey, here's how the bozos got here!"

One of the cowboys appeared from behind the barn, leading the mule.

"Ain't this the critter we snatched?" Snide asked. "We'll use him to carry more dynamite," he added with an evil grin at the boys. "Well, we can't waste any more time with these kids. We got to get moving."

"Where to, boss?"

"We'll hit the swamp and check up on the oil rig stuff. I have to look over all that equipment before we can start drilling."

Frank was thrown over the front of Snide's horse, and Joe against the pommel of a cowboy's mount. Doubled up in this uncomfortable manner, they were carried toward Wildcat Swamp. The horses jogged along at a speedy pace, with the boys taking the bumps and jolts as best they could.

Once or twice Frank tried to ask questions, but Snide cut him off rudely.

"Shut up and stay shut up!" he was told.

By the time they had come in view of the ridge overlooking the swamp, the boys were aching in every muscle. But if they had any hopes of being freed, or even of having their bonds loosened, they soon found that they were doomed to disappointment.

"Keep these kids tied up," Snide ordered, "and haul 'em down with us."

The party descended from the narrow ledge toward the pit in which the fossils lay. There, still firmly in place, was the ominous sign: DANGER. EXPLOSIVES BURIED.

"One move out of you guys, and you're dead pigeons," Snide warned. "This place is loaded."

Dragged from the horses, Frank and Joe were secured to two upright shafts of rock, as useful as tree trunks for tying up prisoners. The boys were made to sit down on the ground, with their backs against the rock shafts, and Snide personally made certain that their bonds would hold.

In plain sight, across the swamp, sloped the heavily wooded mountain. Barely jutting above it, like a tiny cheesebox, was the old fire tower.

Frank and Joe, spotting it at the same moment, shared the same flash of understanding. This must be the tower Willie had mentioned back at the sheriff's ranch.

Twisting slightly, Joe tried to catch Frank's eye. But the movement arrested Snide's attention.

"Listen," he growled, "I warned you two about moving around. Cut it out! We want you alive when your father gets here. Then we'll take all three of you to the tower and—"

BOOM!

The blast of sound mushroomed up between the hills that surrounded Wildcat Swamp like a clap of thunder, bouncing first off one slope and then another, and echoing and re-echoing over the valley. With the reverberation, Snide's flat nose purpled in growing anger.

"What idiot set off that dynamite ahead of time?"

he roared as he looked across at the mountain. "I'll break his fool neck."

"Not *that* fool's neck," one of the cowboys said with a mean smirk. "He probably blew himself to bits."

"Yeah? Well, we're lucky that mountain's still there! What you cowpokes don't know about explosives would fill a book!"

"Don't get upset, Snide," the cowboy said reassuringly. "There's plenty more dynamite left."

"I'll check on that myself," Snide returned importantly. "I have to look over the rest of the riggin' anyway. And maybe we won't put off the business of the tower any more, either. We can take care of the Hardys another way."

The outlaws mounted their horses, and, riding down the slope toward the edge of the swamp, soon were out of sight.

Frank and Joe looked at each other hopefully. "If they stay away long enough, Cap and Chet may come here and rescue us," Joe ventured.

"I sure hope so!" Frank said.

"Do you believe that stuff about explosives being buried here?" Joe queried.

"It's hard to know what to believe," Frank replied. "These scoundrels certainly aren't worrying about saving an old bunch of camel bones, even if it is a fossil."

"I'll bet there's no dynamite here. They sure

didn't seem to walk around very carefully," Joe observed. "And even if there is dynamite buried here I don't believe it can be set off just by stepping on it. They were hoping to scare us into sitting still."

"I guess you're right—and that means we can try to get loose!"

Encouraged by this idea, they struggled hard with their bonds.

"Try rubbing the wire up and down on the rock," Joe suggested. "Maybe it'll snap."

But this was a hopeless effort. Every movement they made only rubbed skin off their wrists. Joe kept hoping Chet and Cap would arrive. But time dragged on and nobody came.

Frank, meanwhile, had lapsed into thoughtful silence. He began going over the entire mystery, step by step. When his mind conjured up the picture of the three phony rangers, dressed in their ill-fitting uniforms, he suddenly exclaimed:

"Joe, we have to get over to that tower, pronto!"

"Why?"

"I have a hunch the situation there is pretty desperate," Frank said excitedly. "From what Snide said, I figure three real rangers are imprisoned in that old fire tower—and Sheriff Paul, too!"

"I get it," Joe said. "The men whose uniforms they stole."

"Right," Frank continued, "and after Willie got all the papers signed, the rangers were going to be released. But not now. I think we've forced their hand."

"How?"

"We came along and found out what's going on," Frank reasoned. "Now those thieves will have to do away with every one of us. So, because of us, those rangers and the sheriff are going to be blown sky-high."

CHAPTER XXIV

Rescue

CAP and Chet, meanwhile, still sore and stiff after
their long captivity in the cave, were riding toward
the Sanderson ranch house. Approaching it, Chet
pointed to a horse tethered in front of the place.

"That's not Harry's," he said, reining in.

"Then we'd better find out who's here before we
barge in," Cap decided. "I've reached the point
where I look before I leap, now, thanks to a tip
from the Hardys."

"If we tie our horses among these trees," Chet
suggested, "we can slip up to the house from the
other side of the barn and look in."

It took several minutes for them to circle around
and approach the place from its blind side. Peering
from the shadow of the adjacent barn, neither Cap
nor Chet could see anyone. Stealthily, they tiptoed
across the yard into the protection of the ranch-
house wall. Flattened against it, they crept toward
an open window.

"I'll look inside," Cap whispered.

Cautiously he raised his head until his eyes were on a level with the sill, and gazed into the Sanderson living room. Almost immediately he ducked, turned, and waved to Chet to take a look.

Chet's hurried glance revealed Willie the Penman, seated at a table with Mrs. Sanderson. The forger was handing her a pen.

"You may as well sign this document," Willie was saying, "and get it over with."

"Oh, I wish my husband were still alive!" Mrs. Sanderson sobbed. "He'd know what to do."

"Harry says it's best," came Willie's high-pitched tones. "And he talked it over with those Hardy kids. They all agree it's the only course open to you."

Cap's hand tightened on Chet's shoulder. The science teacher pointed to the ranch-house door, standing ajar. Silently they crept to the entrance.

"Oh, all right, give me the pen. I'll sign," they heard the bewildered woman say resignedly.

"Now!" Cap commanded, and charged into the house with Chet behind him.

Like twin thunderbolts, they landed on Willie's back. Surprised, the wily forger tried desperately to pull his gun. But Chet knocked it across the room. Ten seconds later Willie was stretched out helpless on the floor.

"Don't be frightened!" Cap told Harry's terrified mother. "We're friends of the Hardy boys," and he introduced himself and Chet. "This forger," he went on, "has been trying to bilk you out of your land."

After Cap had explained the situation to Mrs. Sanderson, the woman burst into tears of relief. Now she would not lose her land!

"Have you seen Harry?" she asked with a worried look.

Before Cap or Chet could answer, Willie suddenly spoke up. "I know where he is," he whined. "He's in trouble; that's where he is. And so are Frank and Joe Hardy."

"Where are they?" Cap demanded.

"Will you let me go if I tell you?" the ex-convict tried to bargain. "Give me a half-hour's start, and I promise I won't go back to the gang. I'll get out of this country fast. And I'll tell you how to save the three kids."

Cap and Chet looked at each other, then at Mrs. Sanderson.

"Can we believe him?" she asked.

"I wouldn't trust this man any further than I could throw him!" Chet cried. "He'd go right to the gang and warn them, and there's no telling what they'd do to our friends."

"I'm afraid he's right," Cap said to Mrs. Sanderson.

She was about to reply when there was the sound of hoofbeats outside. Hurrying to the window, the woman exclaimed, "It's Mrs. Paul and two deputies!"

After being welcomed at the door, the sheriff's wife said she was searching for her husband. "I'm afraid he's lying hurt somewhere, so I asked Bill and Ted to help me find him."

"Why don't you stay with me?" Mrs. Sanderson invited. "Bill and Ted can take this forger to Red Butte and lock him up."

Cap, who did not put much stock in Willie's dire assertion, nevertheless asked the deputies to find out if the Hardys had reached Red Butte. He and Chet would go back to the fossil pit in case Frank and Joe should return and become alarmed over their absence.

"And please look for Harry," Mrs. Sanderson added.

The officers nodded and left with their glowering prisoner. Chet asked Mrs. Sanderson if they might borrow some tools, and after getting them, he and Cap started for the fossil area.

Meanwhile, Frank and Joe, sitting against the rocks to which they were bound, heard furtive footsteps in the defile above them.

"Somebody's coming!" Joe warned.

If it were a new foe, the boys were powerless to defend themselves. Listening intently, they heard the clatter of a dislodged stone. Then, as a head came cautiously into view around the ledge of rock, Frank and Joe shouted in relief.

"Harry Sanderson! Hurry up and untie us!"

While untwisting the brothers' wire bonds, Harry

was told what had happened to them. Then he in turn related the story of his own capture.

"How'd you get loose?" Frank asked.

"Rolled off my horse and cut the ropes on a sharp rock. It was so far to Red Butte that I figured it would be too late to get help to you boys. So I rode back to the Paul ranch. When I saw all the hoof-prints headed this way, I was sure you were prisoners, so I came along. What'll I do now?"

After the Hardys had brought Harry up to date on the news about Willie, Joe pointed to the lookout tower.

"Our problem," he said, "is to get to that place without horses. We think the sheriff and three rangers are being held up there."

"It's not as great a problem as you think," Harry said. "I know a safe way through the swamp. Follow me." He hid his horse in a thicket and set out on foot.

Harry's route to the tower was surprisingly short. He seemed to have an uncanny knowledge of the bog, leading the Hardys along high spots and across a series of hummocks. Soon the three stood at the foot of the tower-topped mountain and paused to look up.

It seemed like an impossible climb, but the boys started up the steep slope on hands and knees. Sharp rocks cut their boots, and saplings which they grabbed for support pulled out of the thin soil. Damp from exertion, the boys finally clambered to the flat stretch of ground on which the tower was built.

The gray, rickety wooden structure, standing in the center of a clearing bounded by scrubby trees, seemed deserted. Panes of glass were missing from the windows around the tower's observation room.

The boys looked about for possible guards, but none were in sight. Cautiously, the three advanced into the clearing and went to the door in the base of the tower. It had been forced open and hung by one hinge.

Frank and Joe stepped gingerly inside. Harry followed.

"Stand guard just inside the door while we go up," Frank told the boy. "Yell if anyone shows up, then run to a safe place."

Harry took up a position behind the broken door, as Frank and Joe started to climb the creaking wooden stairway.

"I hope these steps hold us, Joe!"

The stairs clung to the wall, ascending in steep, right-angled turns. At each step the Hardys took, the tower trembled. Once Joe glanced down over the spindly railing and saw Harry looking up anxiously at them.

"Be careful," he whispered.

The stairs opened finally on the floor of the observation tower. No one was there.

"Guess we were wrong," said Joe.

"Maybe not."

Gazing at the ceiling, Frank noticed that the boards did not match exactly.

"Joe! I believe there's a trap door up there! Give me a boost."

As Frank climbed to Joe's shoulders, there was a sudden pounding above him. Then muffled cries of "HELP! HELP!"

Frank put his shoulder against the trap door and heaved. It yielded and he pulled himself up through the opening.

A strange sight greeted him. On the floor lay four unshaven, disheveled men, securely bound, but without gags. Three of them wore ill-fitting shirts and trousers. The fourth, a blond, ruddy man, was dressed in blue levis and a plaid shirt with a sheriff's silver star on it. Alongside them were scattered crusts of bread and a bucket of water.

As Frank pulled Joe up through the opening, the man with the star greeted them weakly. "I'm Sheriff Paul. These men are rangers."

"We're Frank and Joe Hardy. You have to get out of here—fast! The tower may be blown up any minute!"

With lightning speed, they unbound the prisoners and helped them down to the observation tower. The released men, hardly able to stand, crawled down the stairway.

As they made the perilous descent, Frank and Joe asked, "Who brought you here, Sheriff?"

"I didn't recognize them behind their masks, even when they came close enough to steal the rangers' uniforms. All I know is that I received a phone call about a holdup. When I went to investigate, the three men jumped me."

"Our dad's been captured, too," Frank said as they neared the base of the tower. "He was after a gang of train robbers when they got him."

"Fenton Hardy your dad?" When the boys nodded, Sheriff Paul said warmly, "Mr. Hardy has a great reputation among us law-enforcement men. I sure hope no harm has come to him."

The minutes required to reach the bottom of the tower seemed like hours, but finally Joe hit the last step. Harry's eyes popped as he recognized the sheriff and the rangers. When the boy reported that nobody had come in view, Frank urged, "Quick! Run for it. This place may be dynamited any minute!"

No sooner had they dashed through the doorway to the edge of the clearing than they heard an ominous rumble.

"Down!" Frank shouted. "Cover up!"

As they pitched themselves headlong, the earth behind them split open with a shattering roar. The tower bulged at the bottom and started to collapse.

CHAPTER XXV

Schemers and Skeletons

"Safe!"

Sheriff Paul's whisper broke the silence after the tremendous blast and crash of the tower.

As they all looked back in awe at the mass of debris, one of the rangers said, "If we'd even been in the clearing, we might have been killed."

"The danger isn't over yet," Sheriff Paul reminded them. "That gang will be coming up to check on their job. Let's put some distance between them and us!"

Hurriedly, the little group moved cautiously down the steep slope, finally stopping to rest in a quiet glade near the base of the mountain.

"With Chet and Cap out of the cave, the next step is to find Dad," Frank proposed.

Then the brothers told about their escape from the refrigerator car, the train wreck, and the capture of one of the truck drivers. When they related how they had persuaded Charlie, the driver's assistant, to help them, the sheriff showed keen interest.

"Charlie, you say his name is? Say, that might be Brace, one of the local boys here."

After the Hardys had described their new ally, the sheriff nodded. "That's Charlie, all right. A nice young fellow, but he's been getting mixed up with a bad crowd lately."

"Well, now he's going straight," Joe said. "At least we hope he is."

Discussing the circumstances, all agreed that the next move should be toward the cache of oil drilling equipment.

"No doubt we'll find some of the gang there," the sheriff observed, "and maybe we can surprise them and nab them a few at a time."

They had barely started in the direction of the gang's stock pile when they heard the distant rumble of a motor.

"Sounds like a heavy truck," Joe said.

"Must be on that old logging trail over the next rise," the sheriff ventured. "Hurry. We'll see who it is."

Careful to conceal themselves in the natural cover, they reached the old trail in time to see a truck stop a short distance away. The driver hopped out.

"Charlie!" the Hardys gasped, and Sheriff Paul

nodded. Had he kept his promise, the boys wondered as they watched his actions.

The young fellow seemed to be waving at someone he could see through the trees, but who was hidden from their view. However, they didn't have long to wait, for almost immediately four men emerged from the woods to join Charlie in the road.

Turk, Snide, and two others!

For a couple of minutes the five men stood talking in the center of the road.

Suddenly the back gate of the truck fell with a clatter—and out poured a swarm of men!

Frank's eye caught the foremost of the new arrivals. "Dad!" he shouted.

"Jack Wayne and Sam Radley!" Joe yelled in astonishment.

At the same time the detective's posse surrounded Snide and his three thugs, disarming them and snapping handcuffs on each of them.

Charlie had kept his promise!

Overjoyed, the onlookers left their hiding place. For a moment, all was confusion as Fenton Hardy greeted his sons and their friends.

"But, Dad, we thought you were hurt!" Frank exclaimed.

"No. Jack and I had a rough time, but we won the fight at the plane. Then I made Flint broadcast the story about our capture, to throw the rest of the gang off. Flint's in jail, and so is Snake Fliegel."

"Who's Fliegel?" Frank asked.

Stepping forward with a smile, Charlie Brace said, "Don't you know him? Fliegel is the one who followed you from Bayport to Green Sand in his plane."

"The beady-eyed character who slithers along like a snake!" Joe exclaimed.

"That's the guy," Charlie continued. "He was in with Flint and Willie long before any of us local chaps got mixed up in the affair. Flint told me the whole story."

"How'd he get started after the oil?" Frank wanted to know.

"Flint used to travel around the country a lot," Charlie explained, "riding the rails and scratching out a living where he could. He was doing pretty well in a small town somewhere in the West when he ran into a sick, old wildcatter."

Turk glared at the man who was turning state's evidence, but Charlie continued:

"This old fellow claimed his memory had just returned after a long siege of illness. He was broke, but he said that if Flint would stake him until he could get a job he would tell Flint a tale that might make him rich."

"And Flint believed him?" Joe asked.

"He figured it was worth a gamble," Charlie said. "Anyway, the old man told Flint that fifty years before he had been one of a group of wildcatters who had found a rich deposit of oil. But they had had bad luck. A cave in buried twenty of 'em. Only the old man escaped."

"So that's what the sign meant," Frank said.

"Yes. The poor wildcatter nailed the sign over his friends' common grave. Th shock was too much for him, though, and he lost   memory."

All the listeners crowde close around Charlie to hear the fantastic story.

"After Flint had staked him to a pla e to live and had stocked it with food, the old man led him to the spot—the place you've been calling Wildcat Swamp. Shortly after that, the poor chap died.

"Before he could do anything about the oil, Flint was caught in a train robbery and was sent to prison. That's where he met Willie."

"I wonder why he decided to share the loot with that creep," Joe remarked.

"Well," Charlie said, "I guess he figured Willie would be able to forge the documents to get the land away from Mrs. Sanderson. Then they added Turk to the 'team' because his knowledge of radio would come in handy."

"How did Snide fit in?" asked Joe with a glance at the glowering captive.

"He was an old friend of Willie's and an experi-enced oil man. They contacted him and he brought Fliegel in with him. They gave Snake the job of trying to stop you and Cap Bailey from finding the swamp. He was the one who tampered with your plane so it would crack up before you got off the ground."

"Jack outfoxed them on that one." Joe grinned and saluted Wayne.

"Yes," Charlie said, smiling. "When he flew off and left you at Green Sand Lake, Flint and Turk didn't know what to make of it. They followed you in Fliegel's plane, and Snake was on hand to help them break out of the jail there. Then he piloted them to a field outside Red Butte."

"That's where we came in," one of the rangers spoke up. "We saw his plane land and noticed it had no license number. We investigated and found these cowboy friends of Snide's meeting the plane. Our sudden interest must have scared them."

"Right," said another ranger. "They held us at gun point, stole our uniforms, and shut us up in that old tower until you Hardy boys found us."

"Don't blame it all on us," Turk snapped. "The cowpokes had plenty to do with this deal. They toppled that big boulder over, and sent the fake message to the sheriff's office. Then they called on his wife and fouled up his radiotelephone, returning later to steal it, so nobody'd use it."

The Hardy boys had listened intently to this recital, as it pieced together various parts of the mystery. A few more questions cleared up the rest of the plot.

They learned that it was Willie and Snide who had read the story about Bailey's fossil hunt and had held up Cap in his car; that it was Snide who had lost the pencil code message they had found; and it was also he who had shot down the antenna balloon. The skeleton, Charlie said, had been planted in the cave to scare off intruders.

After congratulating his sons on solving the mystery, Mr. Hardy said, "We ought to go to the fossil pit now to find out how Cap and Chet are."

Several members of the posse were commissioned to take Snide and his henchmen off to join Flint, Turk, and Fliegel in jail.

Then the rest of the group started for the swamp. They had gone about halfway when they met Mrs. Sanderson and Mrs. Paul riding toward them, both looking very much worried.

"We have good news for you, too," said Mrs. Sanderson. "Your friends Cap and Chet captured Willie the Penman just as he was trying to force me to sign away my property."

When they heard this news Frank and Joe let out a whoop.

"You have nothing more to fear now," Mr. Hardy told Mrs. Sanderson. "I'll be glad to get a reputable oil company to check on the old wildcatters' theory of a large oil deposit here."

Soon the party reached the foot of the sandy slope in which the fossil was buried. There was the sound

or pick and shovel from the pit, and in answer to
Frank's "halloo" two heads popped up over the
rim. Cap and Chet dashed down the incline.

"I certainly am glad to see you all with a whole
skin!" Cap declared as he shook hands with the
Hardys.

The brothers grinned. They had indeed pulled
themselves out of a tight fix. Not many weeks were
to elapse before they again found their lives in
danger while trying to solve the mystery of **THE
CRISSCROSS SHADOW** with Chet playing an important
role.

"But wait till we tell you what's happened here,"
Chet said with pride.

"Now what?" Joe inquired.

"Remember when that explosion went off? Well,
we could feel the earth shaking and heaving way
over here. We happened to look down into the old
cave, and you should see it now."

"It was like a little earthquake," the science
teacher added. "The explosion opened a subter-
ranean cavern as beautiful as any in the whole
world. I've seen a good many of them and few can
compare with this one. It's full of gorgeous stalac-
tites and stalagmites. Mrs. Sanderson, you own a
very valuable piece of property even if it turns out
that there isn't a drop of oil on it."

"Sure, Chet said, "and we were the first sight-
seers. Now I qualify for a job as guide."

"A guide!" Joe needled. "You have a job back home—how about that swimming pool? You never finished it!"

"You fellows all ran out on me," Chet said reproachfully. "After all the help I've been to you, I should think you'd want to dig it for me."

"I'll help you," offered Cap. "I think there might be some fossils in that bog even more valuable than the brachiopods you found!"

Chet's eyes shone.

"Frank, Joe, you heard the man!" he exclaimed. "Let's go!"